"In fewer than 200 pages, Les Edgerton's *Hard Times* offers up sexual deviance, brute violence, misogyny, drunkenness, racism, and an astounding variety of cruelties, from casual to premeditated and horrifying. It is also one of the most Christian books you could read, the theme: When we save others, we also save ourselves. The conclusion validates William Faulkner's statement when he won the Nobel Prize: 'The (writer's) voice need not merely be the record of man, it can be one of the...pillars to help him endure and prevail.' Hard Times, one of the best novels I've read."

—**Mort Castle**, three-time winner of the Bram Stoker Award®
and one of "*21 Leaders in the Arts for the 21st Century*,"
Chicago Sun-Times News Group

"*Hard Times* can take its place alongside any opus. This rural noir tale of beleaguered wife and mother Amelia Critchin captures a delicate innocence and twists it into a darkness that sharpens the edges of credibility. Les Edgerton paints a pastel Monet on page one and adds brushstrokes until a deep, rich Heironymous Bosch appears."

—**Liam Sweeny**, Author, *Miner's Kill*

"I highly recommended *Hard Times* for readers who want to explore how the strange intimacy of danger, violence, and hopelessness affects fundamentally good people. It is clearly a morality play for our times."

—**Libby Fischer Hellmann**, author of *A Bend in the River*

"Les Edgerton's *Hard Times* is a razor-sharp take on how people endure, transporting you to a place you'll be glad you don't live and shoving your face into a reality you'll hope you'll never face. Each chapter ratchets up the tension with well-defined characters, each with their own distinct individual voices, living out lives of violence and despair, circumstance and fate, hope and hatred. It's a riveting, action-packed, page-turner that moves like a freight train on fire heading toward an old rickety wooden bridge just waiting to burn. As a reader and passenger on this train hurtling down the tracks into the darkness of humanity, all you can do is hold on tight, keep turning the pages, and enjoy the ride. And know this: it's a ride you won't soon forget."

—**Kevin Hopps**, Emmy-nominated writer,
*Star Wars Rebels, Lion Guard, The Spectacular Spider-Man,
Animaniacs, Young Justice, Blood and Iron*

"Southern gothic was never so real: gritty, humid, layered with mildew and desperation. A chronicle about the tyranny of ignorance and poverty but also a saga of triumph and hope."

—**Mario Acevedo**, author of the *Felix Gomez* vampire-detective series

"Suspenseful, poignant, full of twists and turns, and the lead character, Amelia Laxault, is a testament to the strength of the human spirit. Highly recommended!"

—**Robert Rotstein**, bestselling author of *We the Jury*

"Master of the crime novel, Les Edgerton is back with *Hard Times*, a tale of dust bowl desperation that will shock you and haunt your dreams—or your nightmares. The prose is spare but searing, and while the action starts off like a languid Texas afternoon, the intensity builds until you're left hanging on for dear life to this runaway train of a book. *HARD TIMES* is not to be missed; do yourself a favor and start reading this gem right now."

—**Allan Leverone**, author of *Chasing China White*

"*Hard Times* is unapologetically grim. Edgerton has painted a bleak landscape on a dirty canvas."

—**Dana King**, two-time Shamus Award nominee

"Les Edgerton has a way with drama. From the beginning of *HARD TIMES*, he sets the valuable tone of "what happens next?" and the reader is caught in the web of his amazing story (even if the plan the reader has in mind is merely to browse). Edgerton is a master of suspense, and yet, at the same time, can create sympathetic and complex characters in this labyrinth of hard times. This is a book that can be read from cover to cover in an afternoon because the drama leads the reader by the nose into turning the pages when other things need to be done. One can't help but wonder: "What happens next?"

—**Phyllis Barber**, author of *The Desert Between Us* and *How I Got Cultured: A Nevada Memoir*

"Les Edgerton, the romantic, tells a truly believable story of a folks found in the backwater shallows of America that will twist your soul before winning your heart".

—**Gregory Randall**, author of *St. Petersburg White*

HARD TIMES

"*Hard Times* starts off as a gritty Southern drama, but sneaks up on you as it becomes the type of horror novel that Stephen King and Stewart O'Nan might've collaborated on. Riveting, but not for the squeamish!"

—**Dave Zeltserman**, author of *Small Crimes*

"*Hard Times* is just that: the stiff, unforgiving but poignant life of Amelia. An honor-bound and hardened woman, who, with her quiet dignity is dealing with the hand she's dealt. Forced to trade the man she loves for a sham marriage and the excuse for a life he builds for her, Amelia is pushed beyond her limits when a weeks-long drought turns their world into an absolute nightmare. Edgerton presents her with his trademark storyteller's voice; crisp, unflinching and to-the-point without sacrificing the love one must have to sculpt a novel."

—**Ryan Sayles**, author of *Together They Were Crimson* and the Richard Dean Buckner series

"Read *Hard Times*. For me, it's a five-star keeper."

—**B.R. Stateham**, author of *Lenny*

"Les Edgerton's *Hard Times* drew me in right away to a world that is totally foreign to me, but somehow familiar. That speaks to Edgerton's incredible talent as a story teller. This novel of chapters that stand on their own as short stories reminded me immediately of Tim O'Brien's *The Things They Carried*, and it is just as masterfully written. One of the best novels of the year in my view."

—**Vincent Zandri**, New York Time bestselling, ITW Thriller Award-winning author of *The Remains* and *The Girl Who Wasn't There*

"A lurid, literary tone poem conveyed free of dialogue yet eloquently expressed, vividly vivisecting sultry slices of morally impoverished life in a rural hellhole with stark, sharp, simple strokes of storytelling skill. These characters—whether victims or violators—breathe their burdens right down our necks, sending chills of familiar despair down our spines, since the pitfalls of the human condition are not confined to any particular region or race. Les Edgerton hasn't just read about *Hard Times*. He's lived them to the fullest, and he brings this raw, real life experience to bear with universally relatable flair."

—**Will Viharo**, author of *The Thrillville Pulp Fiction Collection* and the *Vic Valentine, Private Eye* series

"Life among the poorest of the poor in Depression-era East Texas is anything but pretty. In Les Edgerton's *Hard Times*, it's grisly, nightmarish, brutal, and gory. If you've read Les Edgerton, you know he punches with both hands. If you're reading him for the first time, be warned! *Hard Times* is no tale for the squeamish. If you do take the ride, buckle up, hold on to your hat. The story powers along like a runaway locomotive. You won't have a moment to take a breath."

—**Con Lehane**, author of the *Murder Off the Page*

"A tragic tale set against a dark chapter of the American South."

—**C. J. Edwards**, host of the upcoming *Killer Tales* Podcast

"A spare, brutal tale peopled by some of the most loathsome characters you'll ever meet—and some of the most heroic. If readers want to get to know the America presidents from Reagan to Trump keep promising is coming back—and learn why it can't and shouldn't—they will read Les Edgerton's latest. *Hard Times* is a small masterpiece."

—**Jenny Milchman**, *USA Today* bestselling and Mary Higgins Clark Award-winning author of *Cover of Snow* and *The Second Mother*

"Redemption and resilience. Hardships and hope. *Hard Times* is Edgerton at his finest."

—**Maegan Beaumont**, award-winning author of *Carved in Darkness*

"Practically every scene in *Hard Times* earns the book its title. As purposefully as Thomas Hardy or David Adams Richards, Les Edgerton plunks his characters in a dark place and grinds them down page by page, taking them beyond the imaginable. With authenticity and an economy of language, Edgerton makes a horrifying time and place feel uncomfortably familiar. He displays simple human resilience with imagery and emotion that won't be easy to forget, and proves hope exists in even the most dismal corners of our world."

—**Rob Brunet**, author of *Stinking Rich*

"Les Edgerton's *Hard Times* is a powerful, moving, and unflinching look at the lives of ordinary people who are pushed to the edge of a precipice."

—**Paul Brazill**, author of *MAN OF THE WORLD* and other noir novels and series

"Les Edgerton's *Hard Times* wins the award for Understated Title of the Year. He introduces us to Amelia, a young girl allowed a taste of triumph before forces beyond her control compel her into a grim life of struggle and disappointment. The author's distanced prose creates an air of folklore establishing a belief within the reader that this is a common American tragedy. It has taken place before. It's taking place right now. And it will take place in the future. As the story moves into the realm of thriller, the prose picks up the pace and carries us through a whirlwind of action that feels as though it will never let up. The story's antagonist provides sturdy opposition to those united to defend the doomed Amelia. The author presents the most horrid moments in Amelia's life with unnerving objectivity, making the proceedings all the more realistic and all the more heartbreaking. It's often hyperbole to suggest it will be impossible to put a book down, but I think readers will indeed find that task difficult in this instance as they quietly hope Amelia experiences at least a sliver of sunlight before the final sentence of her story is told."

—**Alec Cizak**, author of *Lake County Incidents* and *Cool It Down*

"With the scope of *On the Road*, and the tension of *The End of a Primitive*, Les Edgerton's *Hard Times* arrives at the cookout with Chester Himes and Jack Kerouac already at the card table."

—**Danny Gardner**, Anthony Award-winning author,
A Negro and an Ofay and *Ace Boon Coon*

Bronzeville Books Inc.
269 S. Beverly Drive, #202
Beverly Hills, CA 90212
www.bronzevillebooks.com

Library of Congress Control Number: 2020944035

ISBN 978-1-952427-09-1 hardcover
ISBN 978-1-952427-08-4 paperback
ISBN 978-1-952427-10-7 ebook

10 9 8 7 6 5 4 3 2 1

HARD TIMES

LES EDGERTON

BRONZEVILLE™

— BOOKS —

*To two remarkable women in my life. My late grandmother,
Louise Vincent, who turned out to be the only true parent
in my life. Thanks to her remarkable library that led me to a
lifetime love of books and writing and her unconditional love,
I was given a wonderful model in counterpoint to the man and
woman who called themselves my parents...but weren't.*

*The other remarkable woman is the love of my life, my wife Mary.
None of what I've achieved in life would have been possible without
her and more importantly, nothing that is of value within me
would be possible without her. She is my everything.*

I hold a beast, an angel and a madman in me.
—Dylan Thomas

Arithmetic Prize

Once, in Miss Wexler's third grade, Amelia Laxault won the arithmetic prize. She got a certificate and a gold fountain pen from Miss Wexler and a bloody nose from Arnold Critchin, who caught her on her way home, jumping out from behind a thicket of blackberry bushes along Boudreaux Creek, about a mile from her place. Before she knew what was happening, he hit her, grabbed the paper, and ripped it in two.

Why'd you do that? she said, getting back up, brushing dirt off her shirt with one hand, wiping blood from her nose on the back of her other arm. She doubled up her fist and took a step toward the boy.

'Cause, Arnold said. Stupid girl. He glared at her and threw down the pieces of the certificate and ran back the other way, toward his own home.

Later, out in the privy, she taped it back together and put it in a shoebox she'd hidden out in the woodshed. The next morning, a Saturday, she worked in silence with her mother, taking the shirts her mother kneaded on the scrub board to squeeze out in the rinse tub and put them in the basket to be hung up. When her mother leaned back on her stool for a moment, legs splayed, wiping her forehead with the hem of her dress, she ran to the shed and got the certificate and the pen.

Here, she said, thrusting the mended paper at her. Her mother wiped her face again and pushed up off her stool to stand and read it, a smile gradually softening her mouth as she labored through the words. Amelia held the gold fountain pen up high and the light caught it and both she and her mother gasped at the beauty of it. Read it, Momma, she said, handing it to her.

The pen … she stammered … is might … mightier … than the sword. That's … that's from the Bible, she said.

No, Momma. Mrs. Wexler said it was from a play. An Englishman wrote it.

What's it mean, girl?

I'm not sure, Momma.

Later that night, after her father'd shoveled the last bite of red beans and rice into his mouth and scoured the plate with a piece of cornbread, he told her she was done with school.

What boy would marry a little smart aleck? he said, cheeks bulging with cornbread. You can read, that's enough. He crumpled up the certificate and stuck it in his pocket. She knew better than to say anything. Later that night, when everyone was asleep, she crept into her parents' room, found her father's trousers hanging over a chair, retrieved her certificate and hid it under her pillow with the golden pen that she hadn't shown him. On Monday morning, she went out to the fields with him. He never knew she cried herself to sleep the two nights previous. She did everything he asked, once accidentally slicing the back of her forearm with the machete, cutting sugar cane. He laughed and told her to spit on it.

Rub it in, it'll quit. I ain't gonna kiss it and make it well like yore teacher does, he said, in that voice of his like a saw biting through thick oak planking, and she did. She didn't cry then, and she didn't cry after that for a long time.

***

She dreamed the oddest dream that night. Of a huge black man and a machete. She knew she was dreaming and she made no effort to wake up. She didn't know what the dream meant and she wanted to understand it. Dreams were important in her family. Not the men's so much, but the women's. Her grandmother and her mother both had dreams and they often foretold important things in the future. She hadn't known her grandmother, as she'd passed when she was two years old, but she retained an image of her. An old woman, with long white hair and a mole on her chin with an enormous black hair that sprouted from it. Not a clear picture—more like an image viewed through cheesecloth or plastic sheeting. She'd talked with her mother and her mother assured her it was the correct image. Her mother suggested she'd seen a photograph of her but no such photograph existed when they looked for one. Her mother thought there had been one at one time and it had just become lost. Two-year-olds don't remember like Amelia claimed she had, she said.

In her dream, she was running and it was always the dark of night. All around her were flashes of red, like the eruptions of a volcano, and there were black trees on all sides. Loud barking from dogs filled the air. Just before she woke up, a giant of a black man appeared in her path. He was wielding a huge machete. And then the machete materialized in her own hand and that was the last image she recalled when she woke up and thought about her dream.

She didn't know if the man was there to save her or destroy her.

She didn't know why there were dogs in the dream. They didn't own a dog and she never thought about dogs when she wasn't in her dream. But, there they were and she didn't understand why.

It was a dream that returned again and again through the years. There were other bits added to it in later versions, but the main action remained the same. She never learned if the black man was her savior or her executioner. She never knew what was chasing her but she knew it was something evil and malignant. Awake, she wondered if the black man was hunting her like her father hunted rabbits, with a dog that would chase her in circles until she passed by him with his shotgun. Or in the black man's case, a machete. Maybe that's why there were dogs in the dream.

The other thing that was puzzling was that when she woke she felt oddly at peace. Her mother had no answer for that either, except she thought it was a sign that the black man was there to somehow help her.

Perhaps…

There were many mysteries in life and Amelia assumed this was just one more of those.

A Neighbor Boy

The years passed, the long hot summers spent in the fields tending their cotton and cane from sunup to dusk, and the winters spent tending to their hogs and chickens and the one milk cow as well as her father's mule. Amelia had to do those chores in all seasons, but during the months when the bitter blue northers swept down meant she didn't have to go out into the fields so it became her favorite time of the year. It also meant she was expected to help out her mother with her sewing and household chores along with the livestock jobs, so her workload wasn't really lessened, just changed, but since she got to work side by side with her mother, it was a lot better than having to be out in the fields with her father.

Part of their property was a bottomlands area where Boudreaux Creek meandered through: too wet for cotton and not much better for sugar cane. Whenever they planted cane, it was almost always attacked by a rot, and for several years, her father had just let it lie fallow. One day in her thirteenth year, as it transpired, Amelia's father got the idea to dam up the creek and flood it and try growing rice. Before he flooded it, he planted rice plants he'd nurtured in a small greenhouse he'd built out next to the barn and then opened the dam.

It turned out to be a smart move as the field proved ideal for rice growing.

Her father also showed her how to use a seine to trap minnows from the creek and also showed her how to take the minnows and place each one in a small hole he dug with a trowel beside each rice plant. For fertilizer, he said. There were lots of minnows, almost enough for a third of the plants. It really worked because she could see those plants were always bigger and greener than the plants that didn't get a fish. They both wished there were enough minnows for the entire field, but there weren't. Still, there were a lot.

Eventually, care of the rice field became almost the sole province of Amelia. Her father decided he didn't like trudging through the mud and besides, she seemed to have a genuine green thumb with the rice and she didn't mind the wetness of it all that much.

Besides, she was just a girl and so what choice did she have?

And, something else happened that made her anxious to head out to the rice field each day.

A new neighbor boy appeared one day in the year she was fourteen. His name was Billy Kliber and he and his family had just moved into the old Faulkner place just up the road.

One early summer day, she was out checking on the rice when a tall, fairly handsome, redheaded young boy came walking out of the woods. She instantly liked him. When he smiled and showed off a small gap between his front teeth he didn't seem the least bit self-conscious about it.

Hi. I'm Billy, he said, and then did the totally unexpected. He stuck out his hand and she saw that he was offering to shake hands with her. Good-looking *and* polite! She figured out right away that he wasn't from around there, not with those kinds of manners. She'd never heard of a boy shaking hands with a girl before that moment.

And, he made her laugh. Billy just had a way about him of looking at things from a different vantage point than most folks she knew. It was like he saw the humor in just about everything, even the bad things.

Just think, he said, once they'd told each other about themselves, you could go to China and probably end up being the first woman emperor. I bet they never saw a white gal who could raise rice like you can. They'll think you were an alien goddess set down amongst 'em from up in heaven and will probably want to set up a temple so's they could worship you. You'd end up being the matriarch of the Amelia Dynasty.

She didn't have a clue what he was talking about, but it sounded funny. He sure knew a lot about things outside of the county. China and all! And, he dressed weird. Not in overalls like all the other boys she knew, but regular blue jeans and T-shirts. It seemed kind of risqué to her and she liked that.

Pretty soon, he began coming to the rice field just about every day. She showed him how to raise and lower the dam and why it was important to change the water level from time to time. One of the good things about rice was that, unlike other crops, you didn't have to worry about weeds much. The water level prevented most weeds from getting a toehold. Once they were planted, until the harvest all that was required was minding the water level.

Sometimes they would catch minnows and reach beneath the water and plant them alongside the plants that hadn't received a minnow yet. He liked doing that as much as she did.

That summer was the happiest she remembered ever being. Pretty soon, Billy was showing up at the rice field every day.

And then, the sunshine in her life went away.

It happened one morning when she was lowering the sluice gate to let the water in. Billy was sitting with his back to a tree watching her and cracking jokes when from behind him out popped her father from the dark piney woods bordering the field.

What the hell you sniffin' around my girl for? he thundered, his face black with fury, looking down at the boy. In his hand he was holding his machete.

Billy jumped up like a scalded cat. My name's Billy Kliber. I live over there.

Daddy, this is Billy. He's our neighbor.

I know who he is. Git off my property.

But, sir—

Her father stepped toward him, drew his machete back.

I said, git the hell off my property. Somethin' you don't understand about that, boy?

Billy shrugged, glanced at Amelia, then turned and walked off.

That night, at supper, Amelia tried to talk to her father.

He's a nice, boy, Daddy. Why—

I don't want to talk about that boy, Amelia, he said, cutting her off. He's not one of us. No good will come of that one.

She knew better than to argue with her father. Later, her mother tried to explain. Child, the Klibers aren't like us. Mr. Kliber is some kind of artist. He just rents the old Faulkner place. He don't farm or nothin'. Yore daddy's just tryin' t'look out for yore best interests.

She tried to explain that she liked the boy, but her mother wouldn't listen, just hung her head down and said, You best mind yore daddy. You want to go with boys, you best pick you out one of us. A farmer. Least someone who works with their hands. Those kinds of boys are nothin' but trouble. Lead to nothin' but misery. They don't want but one thing from little girls like you. She didn't ask her mother what that "one thing" was. She was pretty sure she knew.

That didn't mean that was the last of Billy Kliber. Two days later, he came by the rice field.

I don't want your father to chop my head off, he said, laughing when he said it, but his eyes were serious underneath his grin. But I like you, Amelia. That was the first time he kissed her.

The way it worked out, they decided not to chance meeting at the field any more. She'd sneak out, nights, and meet him down by the creek.

As those things transpire, eventually they got around to sex.

It was a Tuesday night and she had just gone to bed. Her parents were already nestled down in their bed in the room next to hers. She was nearly asleep herself when she sat straight up in bed, her eyes wide as saucers, and she nearly screamed. All she could manage was a muffled sound that elicited a response from the other room.

What, Amelia?

It was her father.

A hand over her mouth had kept her from screaming. A hand owned by Billy. Whose eyes glittered mischievously just inches from hers. It took a second to realize he had climbed in her window and was in her bed. He took his hand away.

Amelia?

Nothing, Daddy. I was just having a bad dream.

Well, go to sleep, he said, his voice gruff and irritated.

Yes sir.

She listened, holding her breath, while the bed in the other room creaked. Her father turning over.

After awhile, the sounds died down.

They're sleeping. Maybe, Billy whispered.

What are you doing? she whispered back. She pulled her covers up over the both of them.

He reached over, put his hand on her neck and pulled her to him, his mouth slightly open to receive hers. He had the softest lips, she thought.

He started to give off a little moan, and then stifled it, midway, which caused them both to shake with silent giggles. For some reason, that effort aroused her even more. It must have him as well, from the look that came over his face. This time, she reached for him and drew him to her and their lips came together and she felt like she was falling off a ledge on a very high cliff, but it was a pleasant fall, not at all terrifying. More like floating. He laid back on the bed and pulled her to him, taking extraordinary care not to make a sound and it seemed like the more he tried to remain quiet the more intense his arousal became. It was the same for her.

He kissed her again and opened his eyes briefly and she had hers open as well, and they remained like that, eyes open, hands seeking each other and her body had never felt so focused on a single thing in her entire life.

She felt his fingers on her panties and she felt the air when he slid them down and then his hand was inside and it was incredible, the sensation.

The silence they had to maintain just made everything impossibly delicious. Every movement was in tiny increments as they undressed each other. Her legs opened and he was leaning over her and then he was in her and her legs were around his waist and squeezing and all the time she looked into his eyes, never blinking and they would move together and start to move faster and then both of them knew at the same exact moment that they had to slow it down—their bodies were completely attuned, as one—and they made love that way, slowly, with controlled urgency and when she could stand it no more, he came, and then she came just after he had and while he was in the midst of his passion, and it was like nothing she had ever experienced. No screaming, no speaking, no sound whatsoever, just the silent heaving of both their chests, and they could barely move during any of it, so that it was like every cell in their bodies was screaming above the point where the human ear could hear it.

His hand went over her mouth and hers over his, each feeling the hot breath of the other.

Neither said a word as they lay coupled, and even though Billy had climaxed, his penis stayed hard longer than it ever had and then gradually relaxed and got small and slipped out and it was only then that he eased off her to her side and lay, stomach-down on the bed, his arm across her breasts, her hand warm on his forearm, her breath mingling with his, the perfume of his wet hair in her nostrils.

Five and then ten and then twenty minutes passed before either moved.

Amelia was the first to stir, lifting up on her elbow and gazing down at Billy, who could only shake his head in disbelief.

That was … she started to whisper.

He put a finger to her lips.

No words, he said in a ragged whisper. There are no words.

She nodded and laid her head on his chest and for long minutes they just lay like that. After awhile, as if by mutual, silent consent, they both sat up and put their clothes back on.

Her eyes probed his, darting back and forth, rapidly, searching for a sign in his face of what he was feeling, her own expression one of wariness.

He pulled her down with him onto the bed.

He looked at her with eyes so large and luminous she thought she could easily fall into them and drown.

The only word I can come up with is this. He leaned over, put his mouth to her ear, and whispered.

She pulled back and when she saw his face she felt a happiness flood over her, a kind of joy she had never felt before in this life. She brought up her hand, caressed the side of his face.

I feel the same word, Billy, she said.

They came together, their lips touching, melting together, and this wasn't a bruising, lusty kiss. It was a kiss of sweetness, soft, enveloping, *pure*.

I love you too, Billy, she whispered, her voice husky in his ear, the natural perfume of his hair making her faint with giddiness and delight.

They lay together, not moving, just holding each other, feeling the other's heartbeat against their chests. *No matter whatever happens for the rest of her life,* Amelia thought, *I'll always have this perfect moment.*

They lay together like that for long, delicious moments, and then gradually became aware of sounds and movement coming from Amelia's parents' bedroom. Amelia was the first to stir. She gently pulled Billy's arms from around her, kissed him chastely on his forehead, and sat up.

You've got to go, she said, her face mock serious. Now.

She smiled at his back as he vanished out through her window.

And she imagined the future.

For the next month, she snuck out three or four times a week and they'd meet down by the creek and talk and laugh. And make love.

She was young, three months shy of fifteen, but whereas in the city she'd be considered young, out here in this country, she was marrying age.

And, they talked about just that. She was all for running away right that minute, but Billy talked her out of it. He wanted to finish high school, he said. Probably go to college.

When he said that, she felt sick. If he went to college, there'd be no way he'd ever want a wife with just a third-grade education.

She cried herself to sleep that night when she got back home and snuck back in her bedroom window. She did what had become her habit when stressed. Went over the multiplication tables in her mind. Two times two, equals... She didn't know what to do. She knew she loved Billy, but she knew he wouldn't want an ignorant girl like her forever. She tried out all kinds of fantasies in her mind, but no real answers came to her.

Six times six...

In a way, her fate was decided for her.

Arnold Critchin Takes Amelia to a Dance

The very next day, Arnold Critchin showed up at her house at suppertime. He came to ask her daddy's permission to take her to a dance that was being held the following night at the grade school gym in Cooleyville, the same school both of them had gone to. He didn't ask Amelia, just her father.

Who seemed delighted to give his permission.

She knew better than to refuse her daddy.

So she went.

And, that sealed her fate from that day forward, even though she didn't know it at the time.

Arnold had grown quite a bit since the third grade. He was still skinny, with toothpicks for legs, so thin he looked like a stork, but he'd developed some height, stood just over six feet tall and was still growing. He had a bad haircut, bad teeth, and bad posture. He walked kind of bent over, like he was ashamed of his height.

She was surprised as well as dismayed when he showed up to ask her father for permission to date her. She'd run into Arnold from time to time, mostly during the few times when she went to town with her folks, but they'd never talked or anything. Usually, he was with his friends and did the same as most boys did when they saw a girl. Just hooted and hollered at them, making jokes underneath their breath and then laughing. She always felt uncomfortable around them and mostly tried to avoid them when she could.

When he came by for her the next night, he was polite and quiet in front of her parents, but as soon as they left the house and began walking the three miles toward Cooleyville, his countenance turned surly. He began walking faster and faster and Amelia almost had to run to keep up with him.

Can you slow down some? she said, a few steps behind him.

He turned and glared, but began walking slower. Girls! he said, spitting out the word. Then, seemingly out of nowhere, he grinned at her. Sorry, he said. I ain't used t'walking slow.

It's all right, she said. My legs just aren't as long as your'n. She felt a little better when she saw his smile.

When they got to the dance, they stood up against a wall, watching the folks dance. After a few minutes, Arnold spotted some of his friends and told Amelia, I'll be right back, and went over and began horse-playing with them, hitting each other on the arm and laughing as boys are wont to do. It was the last contact they had until it was time to leave. She saw a girl she used to go to school with and went up to her and began talking and after awhile it was time to go home. They hadn't danced even once. She wondered why he had even wanted to go with her. In a bit, it became clear why.

On the walk home, he was quiet the whole way until they got to the small pine woods near her house. Without any warning, he turned back to her where she was following behind and wrapped his arms around her and pulled her to him.

Arnold! she said. What are you doing?

He snickered. Gettin' a little sugar, he said. It's what you do on a date, y'know. He bent down to kiss her, but she twisted her face away. She tried to break free of his grip but he was stronger. She hit him with her fist, but he'd grown bigger and stronger since she'd tried to hit him that time in the third grade and this time all he did was laugh and punch her so hard in the jaw that she went straight down, dazed and semiconscious.

All she could remember later was his bad breath, panting in her face as he held her down and did his business. She started to cry at one point, but stuffed back the tears, and closed her eyes, enduring. Doing the multiplication tables all during the act.

When it was over, she sat up and pulled her clothes together. Arnold said nothing, just stood and waited for her and when she stood up and began walking toward her house, he followed behind.

You bastard, was all she said. His only response was to grin at her.

Her father was on the porch, smoking his pipe.

Y'all have fun? he said. Amelia didn't even look at him, just walked by and into the house. She heard him and Arnold talking, but couldn't make out the words. They both laughed at something and then it was quiet. She guessed he'd gone. She finally fell asleep with her multiplication tables. Eight times eight, equals sixty-four. Nine times nine…

He came around a week later to ask her to the picture show, but she got out of that by pretending to be sick. That week, Billy had also come by, throwing pebbles at her window until she came and opened it.

You want to come out? he said.

No, she said. I can't, Billy. My daddy will— She didn't get a chance to finish as her bedroom door burst open and there he stood. He strode over to the window. You! You git the hell out of here! She's got a boyfriend. Don't need none'a yore kind sneakin' 'round here. You git now!

Billy's face paled, but he stood his ground. I'd like to hear Amelia say that, he said. Her daddy turned, ran out of the room, and returned a few seconds later, his rifle in his hands. He strode over to the window and shoved the barrel out, pointed at Billy. I ain't tellin' you again, you little pissant! Git off my property.

Billy… She was surprised to hear the word come out of her mouth. Billy, you got to go. I don't want … she hiccupped, swallowed. I don't want you comin' 'round here any more.

He stood there a long moment, then turned around and shuffled off.

And that was that. The last time she saw him for a long time.

Seven times seven…

A Wedding

Oh, lordy! Amelia's mother had said, when she finally told her. Amelia, yore daddy's gone kill yore poor sweet self. Oh, child!

He didn't, although there was a moment when she wished he had. He only slapped and cuffed her, kicking her hard enough in the side, she thought she'd maybe lose the baby whose existence she'd just revealed, but it was only a bruised rib that eventually healed on its own.

The worst part was marching over to the Critchin place, one of her daddy's hands twisted in her hair, the other grasping the stock of his .40 caliber rifle he'd named "Peacemaker." They got married the same day, soon as the hubbub and cussing died down, over at Justice of the Peace Dunfield's, who did the officiating, drunk as a cow on silage, the bridegroom glaring at the floor the whole time, spitting just before he mumbled, I do. Three days later, she turned fifteen.

After the wedding ceremony, her mother made up a stew and brought out a pound cake she'd baked the night before and both families gathered inside to eat and celebrate. Amelia's father had a surprise. He gave the newlyweds a parcel of land along the south end of his property for a wedding gift. He'd made out the deed transfer in Amelia's name, which Arnold wasn't too happy about, but said little, seeing as how it was a free gift. The next day, he and Arnold and Arnold's father and a couple of Arnold's no-account friends spent the day and erected a three-room cabin that looked like it was falling-down even when it was brand-new. By the time it was done, they were all drunk. A week later, they dug a well along with a pump in the house. It took a while to locate water since the house was on a hill and the water table was pretty far underground. There was no thought given to electricity. Too expensive.

Her mother came outside after the wedding to where Amelia was sitting by herself on the porch. She sat next to her on the swing and after a moment of silence, she put her arm around her daughter and squeezed her gently.

Just try not to argue with him, she said. That's the best advice I can give you. Amelia thought about that for a minute, then said, Is that how you are with Daddy? She knew it was and mostly she felt bad for her mother in the few times she'd argued with him as it meant instant wrath and often a slap across the face, but at this moment she was fully wrapped up with her own situation and what she said was from bitterness, rather than from empathy.

So that's what I got to look forward to? she said. Be his doormat? Like you with Daddy? It was the first time she'd ever seen her mother cry and it shook her. I'm sorry, Mama, she said. She took one of her mother's hands in hers. I know what you did. I know most of the time you spoke out to keep Daddy from jumping on me when I mouthed off. I wish you hadn't done that mostly. Except I was just grateful you stuck up for me. I know what you was doing.

Oh, child! her mother said. It's just the way it is, with women. You'll learn. It's not so bad most of the time. Just try to stay out of their way and you'll be just fine.

Then her mother said something that made her blood curdle. We women have a talent, she said. We know how to endure. It's what we do. It's what we *can* do.

Endure?

That was what she had to look forward to?

And, she knew her mother was right. It was what she had been prepared for all her life. She shivered briefly. Her grandmother would have said a ghost just walked over her grave.

That was the only time her mother and her had had a talk like that. She nodded her head. She didn't want to argue with her. But she didn't know if she could live like her mother had. She'd try, but…

And, it was unreasonable, but she felt an immense anger at Billy. Why hadn't he come and rescued her? She knew the answer—he doubtlessly didn't even know she was getting married. And, once he found out, he'd lose all interest in her. What boy would want a girl who'd been with another man? She felt her anger lessen a bit. That part of her life was over, she decided, accepting what looked like her inescapable fate. Her mother was right about that. It was just a woman's lot to have to behave as they did. She resolved then and there to put Billy out of her mind forever. Time would heal everything she told herself. I was a child then, but I'm a woman now—a *married* woman and it was time to do what the Good Book said, to put away childish things and become a woman.

She got up and walked back into the house with her mother. She went over to where Arnold was sitting at the table with his male friends, all of them already half-drunk.

Hi … honey, she said, haltingly, her cheeks burning. She reached down and planted a quick peck on his cheek. His friends hooted and started making wisecracks about how lucky Arnold was, asked him if he needed any help that night, things like that.

It was all she could do to smile and pat him on the head instead of what she felt like doing—haul off and smack him in the back of his skull with a frying pan. She saw her mother out of the corner of her eye and it took away some of the sinking feeling she was having when she saw her mother's lips soften into a brief smile, her eyes glistening a bit.

Until the cabin was ready, she stayed with Arnold at his folks' house. Once it was ready, the couple moved in, along with Arnold's two bluetick hounds, Rufus and Sandy. Amelia had said very little during all of this, but for the first time she spoke up, when Arnold brought the dogs inside and put down pallets for them to sleep on in the house.

Outside, she said, her head down and eyes lowered, but defiance set to her mouth. I won't have no dogs livin' inside the house. I ain't no white trash.

Surprisingly, Arnold didn't argue. He simply went outside and spent the day building a kennel for them.

Better off out here, anyhow, he said. No self-respectin' dawg wants to be around no woman anyways. Bad enough I gotta be.

That night they had sexual relations. They'd had it every night since the wedding, and the only reason it wasn't rape was that they were man and wife, under the law. This was the first night she hadn't tried to fight him though. Out of gratitude for putting the dogs out. In one respect it was better. She wasn't overcome with embarrassment like she was when they did it at his parents' house with only a thin wall separating them. Where she could hear his father's cough and the squeak of his parents' bed whenever one of them rolled over, nothing compared to the noise Arnold made. In the mornings, she kept her eyes downcast and couldn't look at either of them during breakfast, although she could see Arnold's father looking at her from time to time, a sly grin on his face. She couldn't wait to get out of that house and into their own, for that reason alone.

A Baby Arrives

The baby was born six months later and they named her Amanda, Mandy for short.

A redheaded infant. Everyone was surprised and then Arnold's father disclosed his great-grandmother was a carrottop. Everyone accepted that … except for Amelia, who smiled at the instant she first beheld her child and then began unexpectedly to weep. Her mother quickly spoke up. It's normal for a woman to cry after a hard birth like this. She gave Amelia a glance that Amelia found hard to read but she ceased her tears and began to tend to her baby.

She never told her father that the baby was possibly seeded with a rape. Or that it might have been Billy's. She'd known at the time that Billy wouldn't want her once he found out she and Arnold had had sex—even though it was forced—and she knew her father wouldn't believe her anyway. Besides, Billy had already told her his plans to finish high school and go to college and she knew there was no way he'd want her once she showed up with a kid. Even if it was his. So, she kept what she knew and what she thought to herself and did what her father demanded she do. She really had no choice. It was just the way things were. Less than two months after Mandy was born, she was pregnant again. That one was stillborn after going almost full-term, another little girl. There was no funeral. Arnold just dug a hole away from the house and buried her there with no headstone and no words said over the grave. Later that day, Amelia crept out and went to the graveside and said a prayer. Later, she rolled a large rock over to it to mark the spot.

And that's the way it played out with Amelia and Arnold. After awhile, he demanded sex three or four times a week, and she laid there until he was done grunting and poking at her and then he turned over and went to sleep, snoring. She'd always lay awake awhile shortly after that, gritting her teeth and stuffing back the tears that wanted to come out. At first, she used to think of Billy and what might have been and then she saw there was nothing good to come of thinking like that so she put him out of her mind and tried to be a proper wife.

And then, one day, just after Mandy's first birthday, a few weeks after they buried her second child, Billy came back into her life. Briefly. She was in the backyard, gathering up the wash on a Monday. Mandy was inside, asleep on her small pallet next to her parents' bed. The sun was sliding down in the west and dusk was arriving. A light misty rain began to fall, which was why she was taking in the wash.

Billy was a junior in high school that year. Both she and Arnold would have been in that same class if they'd stayed in school.

She heard the clomp of hooves before Billy hove to on a dun-colored mare. At the sight of him she felt her heart nearly stop, before it began beating fast when he leaped off his horse and shined a big grin at her.

Billy! she exclaimed, giving him back his grin. Then, a dark cloud passed over her features and she frowned and said, You shouldn't be here! You've got to go.

Arnold was somewhere down by Boudreaux Creek, gigging for frogs. But he could return at any moment.

Just wanted to see you, Amelia. See how you were doing. Heard you had a little girl.

Oh, God. Amanda. The last thing she wanted was for Billy to see her child. He wasn't nearly as dense as Arnold and his family were.

I'm fine, she said. You need to go. Now.

Can I see your baby?

What could she do? If she refused, what would he do then? Why did he want to see Mandy? Had he heard something? About her ... hair? She started to tell him something—the baby was down and colicky. If she awoke she'd be up all night—something—but before she could say anything, Arnold appeared.

Without warning there he was, coming around the cabin corner, a croaker sack full of dead frogs in one hand, his gig in the other. He stopped dead in his tracks.

What the fuck you doin' here, asshole?

Nothing, Arnold. Just passing by and thought I'd say hi.

You said it—now git.

Out came Billy's grin again. You know what, Arnold? I'll go if Amelia tells me to. It's her place too, y'know.

She didn't hesitate.

Please go, Billy. Please.

His grin vanished. Okay, then. I guess I'll go.

He turned and put his left hand on his horse's mane and prepared to mount. Only, he didn't make it. With a roar tearing from his throat, Arnold charged him with his gig, drawing it back as he ran. Just as he reached Billy, Billy turned aside and unable to stop, Arnold ran his weapon into the mare, the tines stabbing the animal in the side, whereupon she whinnied loud and lunged forward to get away from the pain.

Without thinking, Billy hit Arnold in the face, knocking him down. Bastard! yelled Arnold and came up, whipping out a Barlow knife from his jeans. You're a dead man! he screamed, and lunged at Billy, who stepped aside at the last possible second, grabbing the arm with the knife and yanking down. Arnold fell, snarling, and Billy smacked him on the back of the head with everything he had. The pain in his hand told him he'd broken at least two of his fingers, but there was no time to think about that. Arnold got up on one knee and started to rise, the knife still in his hand. Billy reacted, kicking him in the gonads as hard as he could and down Arnold went, screaming in pain and rage. Billy jumped on him and grabbed the hand with the knife and twisted savagely and the knife dropped to the ground.

Git off'a me, you bastard, he said. Seeing he'd won, Billy got to his feet. As soon as he stood, Arnold whipped his leg around, catching Billy at his knees. Arnold began scrambling around, looking for his knife. Just as he found it, Billy leaped on him and hit him again in the face, causing Arnold to lose his knife again. This time he knew his fingers were broken.

You broke my nose! Arnold screamed. Billy drew his left arm back to hit him again and Arnold yelled, I give up.

Billy stared at him for a second and then said, I don't care. And your nose ain't broke. Yet. He hit him again, with his left fist this time and this time Arnold went out. Billy sat atop him a minute and said to the unconscious man. *Now* your nose is broken, you nitwit.

He stood up and walked over to his mare and yanked on the gig, pulling it out. Blood poured from the wound and he patted the mare and spoke to her softly. Gradually, she quieted down and the whites of her eyes disappeared. The flow of blood slowed and ceased.

He turned to Amelia, who hadn't moved since the fight began. You want to come with me? he said.

She didn't say anything for a few seconds, as if she was weighing his words and what they meant. Then, she shook her head. No, she said. He's my husband.

Billy snorted. That doesn't seem to count for much with *him*.

Maybe not, she said. But it does with me.

He walked over to his mare and grabbed the reins. He wasn't going to mount her with her side wounded.

If he ever does anything to you, I want you to get hold of me, he said.

She didn't answer, just cast her eyes downward. As he walked off, he saw her take a step toward her husband, who was just coming to, moaning and trying to sit up. She knelt beside him and helped him rise up.

Billy walked on.

A Rape

Later that night she cooked supper for Arnold and Mandy, but he didn't eat. Just sat on the porch with his hounds gathered around him, taking hits off a quart jar of whiskey.

After she cleaned up the dishes and got Mandy to bed, the cabin door opened and Arnold came in. He still had dried blood on his face from his nose.

C'mere, he said, roughly. He grabbed her by the shoulder and spun her around. He laid his hand on her neck and forced her to lean over the table. She started to cry out and he slapped the back of her head. Hard. Shut up! he said. He reached down and pulled up her dress and yanked down her underpants. He took his hand off her neck to unzip his own trousers and she tried to twist away, but he was too strong for her. He took her from behind and the pain at first made her gasp and nearly faint. She fought the whole time, but to no avail. She tried doing her multiplication tables but this time it didn't work. She bit her lip and then bit all the way through it. Blood ran down her chin, but she didn't stop biting herself. The whole time he was violating her Mandy cried in the corner where she lay in her crib. When he finally rolled off of her, she ran to the corner of the room.

To where she kept her machete. She turned toward him and brought up the weapon with one hand, wiping the blood off her chin with the other.

Don't you ever do that to me again, she said, her voice flat. Or, I'll cut it off and then I'll cut your damned head off.

He snarled and started to step toward her, then seemed to reconsider and instead turned and walked toward the door and out.

She washed herself when he left, cringing every time the cloth touched her. But she didn't cry. When she'd cleaned herself as best she could, she went to the shelf in the kitchen and pulled down a small box. From it she took a needle and a spool of thread and a mirror and began sewing up her lip where she'd bitten through the flesh, flinching each time she pushed the needle in, but making no sound. That done, she went to her baby and picked her up and rocked her to sleep. She kept her machete on the floor beside the rocker.

It was a full week before he touched her again and the sex when he did was rough but it wasn't from behind.

She could deal with that. It was her duty as a wife. At least, that's the way she saw it. It was just the way it was.

She saw to it that she was never again far from her machete.

Arnold Meets Billy

A week after their fight, Billy was sitting on his back porch when Arnold came walking up. He stood up, clenched his fists.

Relax, said Arnold. I got somethin' for ya. He thrust his hand out and Billy saw a crumpled dollar bill and some change in it.

What's this for?

Your horse. Amelia said I stuck her pretty good.

Whaddya you care?

Arnold looked down at his shoes. Never meant to hurt your damned horse. Meant to stick *you*.

Billy took the bill and change.

Thanks, he said, somewhat reluctantly. The vet already took care of her. This is exactly what he charged me.

I know. We're even now. Don't come 'round my place no more. I won't miss next time.

Billy simply nodded and Arnold turned and walked away.

He stood there, watching him go. Maybe he'd misjudged him. A guy who liked animals couldn't be all bad.

Could he?

Arnold Goes to Prison

As the years came and went, Amelia and Arnold settled into their own brand of married life. It wasn't all that different from many other families in their culture. More kids came and some lived and two more died, one at childbirth and one a week after it was born, coming down with a severe case of the croup she couldn't control. They now had the beginnings of a small cemetery of three graves. Arnold actually purchased a small coffin for the one who'd lived a week, a boy. And put wooden crosses on each of them. Amelia and the other kids put wildflowers on the graves from time to time. She secretly gave each of them names, but didn't tell anyone what they were, not even the children.

They scratched out a meager living on the land Amelia's father had given them. It wasn't his best land; in fact, it was his poorest, but it had some value for farming. The problem was, Arnold wasn't much of a farmer. He never rotated the crop, for one thing. It was too high for rice and he stated he didn't much like cotton farming or growing cane. Cotton was backbreaking, stoop work and cane carried many risks, chief among them the risk of cutting oneself severely with a machete and close behind was the risk of being bitten by thick-bodied rattlesnakes or pretty little copperheads. So, he settled upon corn. Corn was without a doubt the easiest crop, work-wise, to grow. You plowed and planted your field, cultivated it until the corn grew too high to take the mule out, and then harvested it. That was about it.

If he'd rotated it with another crop occasionally, say, soybeans or sorghum, the land would have had a chance to recover and renew itself. But he never did once he settled on corn as his choice of crop. Year by year, the land became more and more depleted until the topsoil was nearly gone and the corn that grew was stunted and the crops grew poorer and poorer. He could have helped it with fertilizer but he only bothered to do that once or twice. Again, it was hard work and the smell made his stomach roll.

The last couple of years had hardly been worth the trouble to plant. For a while Arnold got the idea that he could make more money by turning his crop into liquid, namely moonshine, but he wasn't much good at that and he kept getting busted on his deliveries. His old '29 Nash Model 440 four-door sedan with the running boards couldn't outrun a cop on roller skates and after spending several stints in the county jail and one year in the state joint over in Huntsville, he gave up that endeavor.

While he was at Huntsville, somebody stole the Nash. That was the last time they had an automobile.

The year he spent away in prison was the single happiest year of her married life. By that time, they had three children, two girls and a boy, and while their existence was hand-to-mouth, somehow she and the children survived and, to a certain extent, thrived. Thrived because she walked sixteen miles to Sugar Hill a couple of days each week and found part-time jobs cleaning houses. She was also able to solicit customers to give her their dirty clothes for cleaning. She was able to buy half a dozen White Rocks and they soon grew to more than twenty, which meant they always had eggs and occasionally even an old tough layer to throw in the cooking pot.

She also put in a vegetable garden and put the kids that could walk to work in it, weeding it and helping her gather the produce. They had tomatoes, red beans, okra, potatoes, lettuce and corn. They ate good all that year. The best they ever had, before or since.

That was the year Billy came back into her life.

He'd returned home and took up residence in the farm his family had rented when he was a kid. Both his mother and father perished in a highway accident when his mother was driving back to the farm after a week spent in New Orleans where Billy's father had gone to appear at a gallery showing of his art, and found themselves still six hours from home when their normal bed time had come around and after discussing it, they decided to just drive the rest of the way. About one o'clock in the morning, Billy's mother had fallen asleep as they were coming up to a major intersection and their car slid through the four-way and under a semi. Both were dead on the scene and eventually they found Billy where he was staying with a family friend in town and gave him the news that he was now an orphan.

That was when he got a job on the sheriff's and took his inheritance money and used some of it to buy the farm.

The reason he bought the farm? He saw Amelia in Cooleyville on one of his rare trips. She wasn't alone. She had her children with her. It was the first time he'd seen her oldest, Mandy. And instantly he knew. He crossed the street to talk to Amelia and she saw him coming and hustled her brood down the street. He hesitated a moment, wondering if he should pursue her, ask her the obvious question and then made the decision to let her go. It was plain she didn't want to talk to him.

It was also clear to him that Amanda was his child once he saw her hair. He didn't know her name at that time, but after asking around found out the names of all her children from the lady at the hardware store. And their ages. And did the math and figured out conclusively that the girl was his.

When he first figured that out, he started to go over to Arnold's and Amelia's place to confront him. Halfway there, he came to his senses. If Amelia wanted him to know the girl was his and wanted to leave Arnold he had no doubt she was capable of doing just that. He was sure their marriage wasn't ideal by any means, but it was obviously her choice so he needed to respect that.

He decided that even if he couldn't have Amelia and claim the child as his own, he could still keep an eye on them and be there if they ever needed him.

Which was the reason he bought the farm where he'd lived during high school. He explained to those who wondered why he'd have a farm when his work was in town that he planned on making money by sharing the land out for half the crops. But he'd live in the house. He made an arrangement with the Andersons who lived in the next farm over. Mr. Anderson expressed a desire to increase his acreage from the twenty acres he owned and so a deal was struck.

Until Arnold got caught moving 'shine and was sentenced to a three-year bit in Huntsville. With good behavior he could be out in a year.

Billy waited a week after Arnold had been sent up before he made contact with Amelia. And it wasn't direct contact.

No, he began walking over to Boudreaux Creek, to where Amelia had her rice field years before. Where they used to meet. He had no idea if she ever went there or not. It was no longer a rice field. Arnold had tried growing corn on the plot, but it was a pitiful crop.

After a week of going there each late afternoon after work, he'd fallen asleep under a big oak tree by the creek.

He thought he was dreaming when he heard Amelia's voice.

Why do you come here, she was saying, for the second time.

He sat up, eyes wide.

Amelia.

Why do you come here? I've seen you walk down here every day.

All of a sudden he felt guilty, almost dirty.

Just … because…

Just because? Just because why?

He couldn't lie. Because I thought maybe you'd show up someday.

She didn't say anything. Just stood there looking down at him.

I come here to think about you, he said, finally. This was … our place, you know.

Tears sprang to her eyes and she turned away but not before he saw them. He jumped up, strode to her and wrapped his arms around her.

She didn't struggle, but seemed to collapse within herself. He held her tighter.

I'm a married woman, Billy, she said finally.

I know you are, he said. Come. Sit with me. He went back to the tree. She hesitated a second or two and then seemed to decide something and came over and sat down beside him.

I know you don't love him.

She had no answer for that.

I love you, Amelia. I've always loved you.

She bent forward, her face between her knees, and began weeping silently. He leaned forward, put his arm around her shoulders.

No, she said, moving away a bit and shaking him free. I'm a married woman, Billy.

Should I go?

She was quiet for the space of a moment, then looked at him and shook her head. No, I don't want you to go. But I'm married. I need you to respect that.

She stood up. Here's what I'll do. I'll come down when I can. We can talk. But, that's all. You have to promise.

They met several times a week at the creek. Only to talk. From time to time, he brought her groceries, other things. At first she didn't want to accept his gifts, but when he said he would just leave them there to rot or for wild animals to eat, she grudgingly accepted. He seemed to know when they needed food.

He'd started to kiss her one time, but she pulled away and said, No, Billy. I'm a married woman. He knew enough to not argue with her or to try to persuade her to his way of thinking. When Amelia said something it was final. He respected her for her brand of morality even when he disagreed with it. The same thing happened once when he brought up the subject of divorce. It was something she was never going to consider.

One thing that she did talk about. One time only. When he'd brought up the paternity of Amanda.

They were sitting on the bank of the creek. It was a sunny day, not a cloud in the sky. Arnold had been away for three months at the time. The children were up at the cabin, taking a nap.

Amelia, he said. You've got to tell me. Is Amanda my child?

She looked at him the longest time. Finally, she spoke, looking away from him. This is the only time I'll ever talk about this, Billy. Don't ever ask me that again. She looked back into his eyes. Do you understand?

He nodded, started to say something. She reached over, put her finger on his lips. I mean it, Billy.

They were both quiet for a few minutes, and then Amelia began to speak. Billy saw her hands tremble and her voice was shaky when she began.

Billy, I'm a different person than when I was a kid. He started to say something, but the look on her face made him stop.

I'm going to say this one time and that's the end of it. I love you, Billy. I've always loved you. But I'm a married woman now. I made a mistake by marrying Arnold and I know that now. I was young then and I was afraid and even though I knew you loved me, I thought then that if you found out I was pregnant you wouldn't want me. Shhh, she said sharply as he opened his mouth. Not a word.

I was a child and all I knew was I had to obey my folks. If the same thing happened today, I think I'd do something different. In fact, I know I would. But I didn't. I did what I did and now I have to live with it. And I will. Honoring Arnold as my husband is honoring God and His laws. As long as Arnold's alive, I'm his wife. And, he's the father of my children. *All* of them ... and that includes Mandy. Especially Mandy. I know you don't like it. I don't like it either, but it's my decision. I'm asking you to respect that. Please?

Billy sat silent, taking in everything she'd said, looking at the words from all sides.

Finally he nodded.

They sat there for a few more minutes, and then Amelia stood up. She stepped toward Billy, leaned over and kissed him on the forehead.

I'll always love you, Billy, she said. But you've got to get out of my life. And stay out. Please don't come around here any more.

When she walked away, Billy could see the tears in her eyes.

The upshot of all that was that while he enjoyed the reputation of raising first-class coon hounds—dogs with the purest melody of any such dogs in the county—and he often had buyers coming by to look over what he had to sell—the reality was, many times, he didn't have any extra to sell without depleting his breeding stock. And after a while, he got greedy and began breeding the dogs too often so that the bitches started to deliver pups with several kinds of weaknesses such as weak hips. Out of every ten puppies, he might end up with four or five that lived or were strong enough to sell. When they died, he had them ground up into hamburger—or "muttburger" as he called it—and fed the rest of the dogs their own flesh and blood. Amelia often had nightmares about that, but that didn't stop him.

Waste not, want not, he'd recite. That's right out of the Bible.

She couldn't remember the Bible saying that. It seemed more like something she remembered from history class that Ben Franklin or George Washington might have said and had meant something entirely different, but she knew better than to correct him.

The years slid by, one after the other and mostly things stayed the same. Most things.

What did change, it seemed to Amelia when she thought about it, was Arnold's drinking. And how their farm kept shrinking. Some years the corn came in all right and prices were high and she was able to secrete some away for the bad times which she knew would be coming. They did come, like they always had, and what she'd squirreled away helped them get through those times, but it got harder and harder to hide any money since Arnold, first, rarely allowed her to get hold of any of their income and, second, when she was able to go through his pockets and take some of the bills he hadn't drunk up, there just wasn't many good places to hide anything in their tiny cabin that he couldn't and hadn't found. From time to time, things got bad enough that they had to sell off pieces of the farm. It was down to less than half the acreage they'd begun with. He'd sold the chickens a long time ago, so she couldn't depend on their eggs any more or even an old hen to roast.

Finally, she simply gave up. She grew weary of the times they were down to, say, a few handfuls of beans and maybe some cornbread, and came up with a few bills, which he'd jerk from her and maybe slap her just before he walked to town and spent most of it on liquor. He might bring back a loaf of bread and some peanut butter, but most of it went down his gullet. Or he'd spend the extra she came up with on .22 shells and shotgun shells for his .12 gauge and take the dogs out hunting.

They ate a lot of critters. Coons. Possums. Squirrels and rabbits. Every once in awhile an armadillo. They all liked armadillo. It wasn't as greasy as coon and was much more tasty. On one happy day, Arnold and his dogs cornered a wild boar and that lasted them for over two weeks. It was also one of those rare times he laid off the bottle for the most part.

Arnold now had over a dozen dogs. Redbones, blueticks, black-and-tans. A pair of pit bulls he'd just added, alert to the possibilities that breeding fighting dogs presented. He built a pen and a run for them to keep the pits and the hounds separated to prevent the pit bulls from attacking the hounds. Between the expenses for them and the hunting as well as his drinking, Amelia and the kids often went to bed with distended bellies. The only child that looked relatively healthy was Crystal, the new baby who could still suckle milk from her breasts.

Which were rapidly drying up.

It was at this time that the skies became bluer and clearer and the clouds began to wash out of the sky. Along with the rains. The sun seemed to shine more fiercely each day.

One, two, and then three days without any moisture went by.

Then four.

A week and then a second week.

Then a third and still no rain. The temperature rose to and then remained in the high nineties.

More Heat...

She'd cooked all but a little of the rest of the mule, which had lasted almost a month after it broke a leg and had to be put down a couple of months before the drought began. It would have lasted longer but more than half of it spoiled since they had no place to keep it. The meat wasn't beef or chicken, but it could still be choked down. Rank and strong-smelling, it sustained life and that's what was needed. The children stopped playing tag and hide 'n' seek in the yard, any game that required energy or much movement.

Mule meat was all that was left. The chickens had long ago been eaten or sold off as had the other animals that hadn't run off or been killed and eaten by wild animals.

Gathered around the table, too exhausted to even whine, her brood just sat staring at their plates.

Mama, it's spoilt. It's nasty, said Mary.

Hush up and eat it, said Mandy, older than her thirteen years. It's all we got. Don't be such a baby.

We can't! both Mary and Abby wailed, and Amelia picked up a spoon and ladled a bit of the gravy from her own plate into Crystal, the eight-month-old's mouth. The baby promptly threw up. James didn't say anything, but didn't eat either.

That was when Arnold Critchin stood up and snatched up the plates, stacking them in a pile. He carried them out to his dogs, who came whimpering up to the porch, their tails trying to wag down between their legs, one or two of them growling from behind grinning teeth. He'd turned the pit bulls out with the hounds the day before and so far everything was okay. There'd been a couple of minor fights but nothing more. The male pit bull was the one that growled at him, baring his teeth. Buster, he'd named him. He kicked him in the side. The dog snarled but didn't back down. Arnold kicked him again and this time he slunk away, looking back, the red of his eyes showing, a soft snarl from his throat.

That's the kids' food, Amelia cried, running out behind him and bending down to snatch one of the plates from the biggest of the hounds, a black and tan he called T-Bone. The dog almost casually reached over and sank his teeth into her wrist at the same time her man was swinging his fist at the back of her head, knocking her off the porch onto the ground. Back inside, she rubbed the arm she'd used to break her fall and wondered if it were broken or just bruised. She wrapped a piece of kindling tightly around it with a strip of cloth and tried to ignore the ache. It was already swelling up and an angry red. It was the same arm the dog had bitten.

The next morning, when Arnold sat down to the table, he stared at the plate she put silently before him. Save for a tiny bit she had hidden, it was the last of the mule meat. He took one bite, chewed in moody silence for a moment and then spat it out. He picked up his hat from where it lay on the table, clapped it on his head and spoke to Amelia, his voice china egg brittle.

I'm goin t'town, fine some work.

She watched him from the window until he was just a tiny brown insect, far away in the vastness of the red dust. He had gone like this before, and stayed away one or two days, even one or two weeks, but Amelia knew somehow this leaving was different.

Arnold's Been Gone for ... Days?

Amelia woke up. Confused at first, she gradually came to the conclusion that she'd gone to sleep the afternoon before. There was no clock in the cabin and she didn't own a watch, but she estimated it was about ten in the morning. The *following* morning.

Something was wrong and it took several minutes before she figured out what it was.

Silence.

Mid-morning and the cabin was quiet as a crypt. She couldn't remember that ever happening. She looked around and saw her oldest, Mandy, curled up on the floor over by the pie safe. Her hair was plastered to her forehead by her sweat.

She forced her aching body to stand upright and went into the children's bedroom to check on the others. They were all asleep. She considered waking them and discarded that idea. They'd only be hungry and she had little to feed them. Best to let them sleep as long as possible.

And hope Arnold returned with something to eat.

Soon.

***

The kids slept until noon, stirring one by one, coming out into the kitchen to sit listlessly in the chairs around the table. There was a little flour left, about two cupfuls. She took what there was and brown water from the bucket that stood beside the stove and mixed the flour into dough. There was no yeast for leavening or salt for taste. She was careful with the water.

She molded the mixture into four tiny cakes and relit the fire and baked them in the cast-iron skillet, slowly and carefully, as if cooking them too fast would somehow diminish their bulk. When they were done, she put them on a piece of oilcloth and cut each in half. That would be two meals for the children.

She didn't make any for herself. She'd just eat whatever they left.

Mama, you can have mine. I'm not that hungry. James, trying to be the man of the family with his father gone. She smiled at him. She spoke to him, using her pet name for him.

No, Sugarman. You eat, son. We're going to need your strength.

He thought about it a moment and then nodded. She watched him trying to eat slowly to show he wasn't hungry, but she also saw him chewing frantically on each mouthful when he thought she wasn't looking. She gave him a hug. Her Sugarman. It's what she called him when Arnold wasn't around. She'd learned not to call him that when his father was there.

Quit callin him that sissy-ass name. Just put a dress on him, why don'tcha?

But he was her sugarman. As hard as he tried to be like his father—hard and cold—it wasn't in his nature. He was just … sweet.

They'd gone without food before. This time seemed different and she fought the fear rising up in her like a physical thing.

Besides Amelia and the kids, all that stirred on the place were her old man's dogs. A baker's dozen mangy, long-limbed, thirst-tempered hounds, half males and half bitches with one of the females pregnant. And the pair of pit bulls. She had nothing to feed or water them with. But they could walk down to the creek and if it hadn't completely dried up, get a drink there.

Later that day, she took James with her to the creek, followed by most of the dogs, and filled two buckets with water. It was brackish water since the creek wasn't moving and mostly lay in small pools, but it was water and what they needed. They lugged the buckets back and the dogs remained at the creek, lapping water noisily. A while after they got home, the dogs returned to lie around the yard.

That night two things happened. The children ate the last of the flour cakes and what was left of her tiny hoard of meat, and the bitch gave birth to a litter of four pups. Surprisingly, they were all alive.

There was no food left in the house.

After she put the children down that evening, humming to quiet the smallest one's whimperings, she scoured the house in a vain effort, looking for food. Even insects. There wasn't any.

Jail

Way it started off, way he looked when the two deputies came in the front door of Roy's Tap, they didn't even bother to unhook the clasps on their gun holsters, just walked over and bent down to lift him up, one on each side.

Asshole didn't look like he weighed more'n a hunert twenny, hunert thirty pounds, said one of the deputies at the jail an hour later. Li'l ole scrawny arms, 'bout as big round as your Slim Jim, Faustus.

Wasn't his arms did the damage. Lookit this, Ezra. Prolly gimme rabies. I got to get a shot now, mebbe stitches. The one named Faustus held up his forearm. Blood still flowed, seeping into the torn khaki sleeve, teeth marks clearly visible.

Four other officers crowded around them, looking at Faustus's arm. The oldest, a lean, hard man with captain's bars on his shirt, peered at the wound from under the bottoms of his glasses and said, Hell, y'all don't never get outta town much, I reckon, get up in the hills. Y'all did, y'all woulda known that was old man Critchin. Arnold Critchin. He's usta hunting wild hogs with a Bowie knife, couple little bitty city boys like y'all ain't nothing t'him. How long Roy say he been there drinkin? Lessee. He walked into the cell, which hadn't been locked yet, and with the toe of his boot pushed at the lump lying in the middle of the floor. The lump stirred and gave out a little moan and curled itself into a tighter ball. Grimacing, the captain walked back out and clanged the door shut behind him. All day, and probably all last night, I'd say. Left his ol' lady again.

He walked up to the desk near the front of the room, picked up a ring of keys hanging on a nail, and tossed it to Faustus. Lock 'im down. Soon's he sobers up, fine out what he's doin in town. Ask how his ol' lady is. I went to grade school with her. Smart woman. Too good for *him*. He put on his hat and pulled it down low on his forehead, put his hand on the doorknob. Tell this asshole he earned hisself thirty days this time, minimum. Fine out if his wife has any food or money. Last time he went on a binge he left her up there all alone with all them damn dogs and kids and nothin' in the house.

Lord! the other deputies heard him say, going out the door. Ain't it never gonna rain again in this damn place!

No Food, No Water

Sixteen miles away, accessible only by a dirt road for the last twelve, was a pine board cabin, divided into three rooms by brown burlap bags sewn together and strung on a clothesline. No back door and only one window, in the front, but it had a porch of sorts, on which lay panting half a dozen black and tans, a pair of pit bulls that could have been twins, mostly white with dark brown mottling. Another five or six other black-and-tan hounds and Walkers scattered around the yard, all lying down in whatever bit of shade they could locate. If you could call it a yard. Nothing but brown straw that used to be grass, and red dust that swirled in little lazy tornadoes.

The woman sat in her cabin staring out at the hill that was a deeper red than the rest of the land and brushed away a fly buzzing near the back of her head. A praying mantis of a woman, arms and legs protruding sharply at right angles from her body, cheekbones sticking out in stark relief against the lines of her face. In her mid-thirties, although a stranger might have guessed twice that.

Mama, did Daddy go away?

Amelia Critchin pushed a long strand of brown hair mixed with gray back into her clumsy bun, looked at the girl and then away from the sight of skin stretched over the outline of her ribs.

He went to look for work.

Mommy, I'm hungry. Three-year-old Mary, the second youngest, came grade? You remember when Amelia got the math prize? Yeah, she wuz smart, but I wuz smarter. I knew the multiplication tables inside out. That prize shoulda been mine. Only thing, if I'da won it, that woulda been my last day in school. Might as well a been, though. He stared out the window behind the sheriff, his eyes fixed on some point outside. Daddy made me quit the next year. Tricked me. Asked me to help him on his tax form. Did the whole thing in ten minutes. Too smart for my own good.

He stood up.

You kin put me back in my cell, he said. You know, Sheriff? Things ever git rough for you? You ever have to sell yore land to feed yore kids? Naw, I don't guess so. Long as they's people t'pay taxes you git yores.

So that makes it okay to beat your wife? That makes it okay to treat those dogs better'n your family? I ain't buyin' it, Critchin. Sam! he said to the deputy over at the filing cabinet, Put this piece of crap back in his cell. Tell Faustus to get on over to his place, check on things.

Sheriff, Eugene and Faustus took that prisoner on down to Houston. They won't be back for two days, minimum. Prolly three.

The minute they get back, then. First thing. Tell them if she ain't got any groceries to get her some. Take it out of Discretionary.

He picked up his hat. First thing when they come back, hear?

How 'bout my dogs. Y'all gonna check on my dogs? My dogs is hungry, too.

He went out, ignoring the man in the cell.

He thought about it awhile and decided that even though Critchin was a piece of shit, he was probably right about Amelia and the kids. She was a survivor and it would be just like her to have food hidden. He figured another couple of days wouldn't hurt before checking on her. It was still worrisome but he shook off the feeling.

Memories

A few minutes later, the sheriff's captain hoisted himself up on a barstool at the now-deserted Roy's Tap. Draft, Roy, he said, and when it was served, he drank half of it down in one long gulp.

Y'all got that asshole locked up, Billy? Roy said.

Yep. I'm kind of worried about Amelia, he said.

Roy looked at him, a question on his face.

You know his old lady?

Indeed, he did. He downed the rest of his beer, then tapped his finger against the mug and Roy fetched him another.

Amelia. It'd been a long time. A lot of miles and a lot of days.

He thought back to when they were kids. When his family had moved to the old Faulkner place from Houston so his father could just paint. Amelia and her rice field. Amelia and that Critchin kid. Her marrying him. Him standing outside her window, asking her to come out and then her daddy appearing, waving his big ol' rifle at him. Remembering being scared out of his britches but standing his ground. Amelia telling him to leave, that she didn't want him coming around any more. The run-in with Arnold a year or so later. All that stuff he'd thought was in his past and forgotten.

Making love with her. That he hadn't forgotten, but sometimes wished he had.

He sighed and drank some more. Christ! He'd been so young then. Full of ideas about going to college and coming back for her. All ruined when she married Arnold Critchin and had a baby. He'd wondered some about that baby and then found out.

He had gone to college. Finished a semester at A&M and then just quit. That old farm, the town, the people had got to him, got in his blood. Books lost the appeal they'd had. There was something about this place…

He knew what that "something" was. Amelia. He could never get her out of his blood. He knew he'd never have her now that she was married, but he couldn't help himself. He had to be near her. For all his smarts, he guessed he was sure some dumb ass.

It didn't matter. He got jobs doing farm work, hired out for some of the lumber mills, day labor, scut work. And then, an opening came up in the Sheriff's Department. Something he'd never considered in a million years, but then he hired on and it just felt right.

Before he'd gone away to college and after he'd had the altercation with Arnold, he and Amelia had had more than one encounter. She rarely came to Sugar Hill, preferring to take her rare trips to Cooleyville as it was much closer and she knew people there from going to grade school there, but on occasion Billy had had business in the smaller town and they'd ended up passing on the street or, even once, had come face to face in the hardware store where Amelia had gone to buy a new whetstone for her machete and Billy had wandered in looking for a new part for his tenant's tractor.

The hardware meeting was during the year Arnold had been sent to Huntsville for his moonshining activities, and when Billy learned she was all alone with her kids on the farm, he made it his business to stop by their cabin about once a month to bring her groceries.

It was during those visits that they got to know each other as adults. Mandy was a small child then and the instant he'd seen her red hair, he'd begun to wonder if she might be his. Finally, one day he just asked Amelia.

She's Arnold's daughter by law, she'd said, adding that was all she was going to say on the matter.

Billy accepted what she was saying. By law, Mandy certainly was Arnold's daughter and not his, but Amelia using the law as her basis for Arnold's fatherhood told him pretty much what he needed to know. Mandy was his daughter. And, even though he couldn't be her father in reality, he could in spirit. Which was why he made it a point to be sure all of them had enough food.

When Arnold came home from the joint, Billy ceased his visits to their place, although from time to time he made an effort to try and run into either Amelia or Mandy, just to ease his own mind as to their welfare.

That had been a long time ago. Both of Billy's parents had died and he ended up buying the Faulkner place, only he didn't live there, didn't farm it. Shared it out and gave the Adams's family good terms and let them have the use of the house. He had a small apartment in Sugar Hill, just a couple of blocks from the jail. It'd been a good arrangement for both him and the Adams's. At his request, the Adams's had kept an eye on the Critchins, and when he collected the rent gave Billy updates on their status.

Until a month ago, when the drought hit and the land dried up and began blowing away and the Adams's had given up and left. He figured when it was over, they'd come back or if not then someone else would come along he could rent it out to.

No one knew why he'd wanted to buy that old place except him. It was because Amelia lived on the next farm. Probably why he'd never married even though he'd come close a time or two.

He tossed bills up on the counter. Thanks, Roy. I'll be seeing you later.

The Mockingbird Café

Saturday nights, Lucious Tremaine went to the Mockingbird Café in New Orleans. He came always by himself and seldom talked to anyone save the bartender and that just to order another drink. The bartender, Fathima, knew more about him than anyone else who frequented the place, not because of any confidences exchanged, but because of two neatly folded together newspaper clippings that had once fallen from Lucious's pocket and were found later by Fathima when he swept up. One clipping was a report of a shooting and a death and a trial and a jail sentence meted out. The other about a convict who had escaped from an Ann Arbor hospital after an operation and a massive transfusion for wounds gotten in a dustup at Jackson Prison. The man had somehow removed catheters and needles from his body and removed his body from the hospital, walking out sometime after midnight, somehow unseen past the guard posted outside. The writer of the second article seemed amazed that such a thing could be done, considering the deleterious physical state the patient was in. There was a brief human-interest sidebar mentioning the man's family—a wife on welfare, and a daughter on a dialysis machine, in Detroit. The subject of both articles was a man named Lee Atwater. Though there was no photograph, the bartender had no doubt they were about the man he knew as Lucious. Fathima kept what he read to himself. He knew lots of secrets. He had a few of his own.

Lucious favored cheap wine and shots of Seagram's 7, which was just fine with the bartender, since that was his stock in trade. You could tell that by the stale air, soon as you stepped inside. If the smell wasn't enough, if you were a heavy smoker or had sinus trouble, then a glance at the backbar at the six or seven bottles there would let you know this was a boozer's kind of establishment, and it didn't pretend to be anything else.

The Mockingbird Café wasn't really that anymore. A café, that is. At one time, yes, you could get a burger, fries, and even a malt that had real malting in it, and a waitress with piled-high hair who called everybody "Hon" and suggested the "red beans and rice—it's real good today," but no more.

There was another Mockingbird Café in New Orleans, not far from this one, and that one was famous and was pointed out to tourists in buses by uniformed guides. That one had rows and rows of bottles on the backbar, all different colors, with heads of shiny stainless steel shot measures, and brisk waitresses and polite college-age bartenders in forest green shirts with tiny white and black birds on the breast pocket. Tourist buses were careful to avoid the street the other Mockingbird was on.

Originally, it had been called "The Sweet Shop," and then the founder and owner, Miz LaFouchette, renamed it after her favorite bird, on the occasion of adding beer and hard alcohol to the fare, because when she was barely a teenaged girl, a boy who sat in front of her in algebra class told her one day she reminded him of a "cute li'l ol' mockin' bird." Then, Miz LaFouchette passed away and Ike Washington had it fifteen years, and then there were six other owners in rapid succession within the following decade while it completed its transmogrification into its adult stage, a honky-tonk.

You had to step to your left halfway back to the bathroom to avoid a hunk of ripped linoleum. You didn't know if the rust stain on the wall above the lone urinal was water damage or blood. It could have been a legitimate source of speculation in the Mockingbird Café, if anyone had cared.

That was how Lucious Tremaine found it and it seemed to suit him.

Life in New Orleans When You're on the Run

In the fifth decade of his life, Lucious Tremaine sat always on the same stool at the far end of the bar, leaving only one possible seat beside him and making it plain with the pitch of his head and the incline of his spine that he wasn't open to socializing. The regulars, wise to this breed of man, kept their distance, omitting him from conversations about the heat or how the ponies were running out at Jefferson Downs, and even the worst of the derelicts bypassed him when sponging drinks. Now and again a Yankee tourist wiping sweat from his brow might stop in by accident, a stray from the tourist paths, and plunk down next to Lucious, and such a person might ask him where the best place for shrimp or girlie-shows was, but Lucious would stare straight ahead and growl in a low, don't-mess-with-me voice, I look like a fuckin' cabbie? and the tourist would slug down his drink or not, and get out, leaving a too-large tip behind.

Where he lived or got his money to drink on, no one knew. Fathima figured he worked in one of the shipyards over in East New Orleans, from a few chance remarks Lucious had made, and from what he deducted were burn marks from a welding rod he'd seen on his forearm once. Some of the smaller shops were fairly casual about background checks, especially if the applicant agreed to less-than-union wages. His clothes were faded and worn but clean, and he fancied a Tulane baseball-style cap. He didn't smoke and he kept dollar bills in a wad in his sock, inside the left work boot. Whenever he put a new bill on the bartop, Fathima would pick it up gingerly with thumb and forefinger, a delicate move for someone who weighed three hundred and fifty pounds and had killed another kid during a high school football game. The crossbody block he threw that killed the kid was legend even beyond the Irish Channel where Fathima was from, but as mean and respected as Fathima was, he never said a word to Lucious as to the sanitary condition of his currency. He might have thought of doing so at one time, but not after he read those clippings. He just put those bills aside in a separate part of the cash drawer and gave them back in change to people he didn't particularly like.

Sometimes Lucious would stare back at the group of men shooting pool as if he wanted to walk back and pick up a cue but he never did, and no one ever asked him to join them.

Tourists and Miss America

It was of a Saturday evening, one of those hot and steamy New Orleans nights when the knives and guns come out a little bit quicker than usual, and Charity Hospital's emergency room looked like a MASH unit, that two tourists stepped through the doors of the Mockingbird. A man and woman, she pretty and dressed in something smart, black and expensive; he small and snarly-looking and black-tied and tuxedoed and the both of them white people. They walked the empty length of the bar and picked the two stools next to Lucious. The cacophony of the bar dissolved and the sound of the last click of balls at the pool table hung in the air for a long, pregnant second as all movement paused and then started up again at a higher intensity.

VO and ginger for me, said the man, and a daiquiri for the lady. He pulled out a bunch of crumpled bills and dropped them on the bar, picking them up one by one and snapping them straight.

No blender, Fathima said, his weight shifting back on his heels, and no VO, and the man didn't get it for a minute and then smiled and came with, Well, then she'll just have a Jack and ginger and the same for me. He settled for Wild Turkey and 7-Up for the both of them, and they had a grin over that, and then they asked Fathima to turn on the TV, as the Miss America pageant was about to begin and there was no way in the world they were going to be able to get back to their hotel in time for it, which is why they had stopped at this fine establishment, the man explaining all this in a loud voice. You could see Fathima considering the request, but then he shrugged and turned and switched on the set and flipped through the channels until he found a crowd of girls in evening gowns. That done, he went down to the other end of the bar and picked up the sports section of the *Times-Picayune.*

Miss Mississippi. It was the tourist lady.

No way. Miss North Carolina. She's a brunette. Mississippi's a blonde. Brunettes always win.

The man and his companion were having a friendly argument. The woman decided to ask Lucious for the tie-breaking vote.

Which one do you like, sir?

At first, he didn't realize they were talking to him and he ignored them, but then the woman patted his arm and asked him the question again.

Don't matter none to me, he said, not looking at her, both elbows on the dark wood of the bar, eyes fixed on a point in front of him.

Oh, come on, sir. Which one you think's the prettiest?

It was the man, leaning around, mouth grinning and eyes shining.

Or most talented. The lady, chipping in.

Look alla same t' me. Look like white folks business t'me.

The noise level in the Mockingbird lowered several decibels. Even those who hadn't heard him could sense something was about to happen.

What, what? someone said, back by the pool table.

It's Lucious, man, someone else said. *He's talkin' t' them white folks.*

Excuse me, sir? It was the white man. He leaned forward farther and peered around the woman, his mouth still smiling, his eyes bright.

It's a joke, Sam. Between the two men, the girl smiled, turning first to beam at Lucious and then at the man she had called Sam.

A joke?

You know how some people think black people all look the same. The gentleman's saying all white people look the same. She kept smiling at both men, back and forth.

Lucious didn't answer, just kept staring ahead, his hand on his drink.

Is that it?

It was the white man, Sam. He was twisted sideways in his seat, his whole arm on the bar, head in hand, looking around the girl at Lucious.

Is that it, sir?

Wasn't no joke.

Lucious didn't turn his head, just stared straight ahead. Up at the front of the bar, Fathima folded his newspaper with exaggerated, noisy motions, then laid it aside, staying where he was, but pointedly staring down the length of the bar at the trio on the other end.

You think we all look alike?

Don't matter what I think.

That's right, podner. It "don't matter" what you think.

Sam. It was the girl. Her voice was small, scared. Sam, let's go.

Sam stood up, looking hard at Lucious, never taking his eyes off him, even though his words were for the woman.

Shut up. Go outside and get us a cab. She didn't move, stayed where she was.

He spoke to Lucious.

You know what I am?

Lucious turned his head for the first time, in the man's direction, but didn't make eye contact and then turned back.

I know what you are.

And what would that be?

You're a cop.

Yeah. The man laughed. Yeah, I'm a cop. I kinda figured you knew. You been in the joint, ain'tcha?

Lucious stood up, picked up his drink and walked around the couple, up toward the front of the bar, and sat down on the farthest stool. He pushed his glass at Fathima. Fathima picked it up and turned around for a bottle of port wine. Lucious reached down and took out a small wad of bills from his sock, extracted one and put the rest back in the sock. Fathima took the dollar bill between his forefinger and thumb and put it in the special drawer. He asked the white couple if they wanted a refill.

When the white man got his drink, he picked it up and walked up to where Lucious was sitting. The girl put her hand on his arm as he got up, but he ignored her. Her face was pale. She remained on her stool.

My name's Sam, said the man when he got to Lucious. He put his hand out and Lucious just stared ahead, at the row of bottles behind the bar. Sam stood there, hand outstretched, then turned his palm up, looked at it, wiped it on his trousers as if it had somehow gotten dirty. He laughed and pulled out the stool next to Lucious and sat down, swinging around so that he faced the black man.

You're not real sociable, are you?

Leave me be.

No, sir, not too sociable, the white man went on, as if he hadn't heard him. Now why would that be? Let's see, you're a big one, look like you could handle yourself. I'm a white guy, in a black bar, kind of gettin' up in your face, if you want to look at it that way … but you, well, you don't do nothin' about it. Now, it could be you just naturally respect the law, but somehow I don't think that's it. You know what I think?

Lucious took a swig of his wine, looked dead ahead, jaw muscles working, but not a word to acknowledge the man was there.

I think there's paper on you. There's a warrant on you, ain't there? You done somethin' real bad, ain't you, ol' son? Now, I ain't from around here, I'm Tennessee law, but I bet I could find me a police around here like t' talk t y'all.

Again, Lucious lifted his glass, took a swallow, stared at the backbar in front of him. The other man slugged down the rest of his drink and slammed the empty glass down on the bar, hard, and got up, swinging his leg wide to clear the stool, like a cowboy getting off his horse. Not an ear in the place heard their exchange, but not an eye had missed it.

The white man walked halfway back to where his girl was still sitting and told Fathima in a loud voice, How 'bout another one, pal, and give my friend here one, too. He winked at the bartender and inclined his head toward where Lucious was sitting.

Lucious got up, drink in hand, and walked around the man and then the girl and back to the rear of the bar, where the pool table was. He sat down on the bench where the kibitzers sat. Even though he sat apart from the couple of men who were already there, they scooched down even farther away from him.

The man called Sam came walking back with a drink in each hand, and sat one of the glasses, a wine highball, down on the ledge just behind Lucious's head.

"Here's our drink, *boy*," he said, and somewhere there was a sharp intake of breath, and for the first time Lucious looked directly at the man.

Before anything could happen, a huge shadow slid between the two men.

Leave it alone, Fathima said to the white man, standing between the two, his back to Lucious. A look, not of fear exactly, more of surprise, passed over the white man's face and then something else, and then it was gone, and he was too, with a loud, strained snort, back to the bar where his woman sat on her stool, twisting a strand of her hair nervously between her fingers.

Fathima waited until the man had reached his companion and then he turned and eyed Lucious, who held his gaze for the briefest of seconds, then looked down and away.

Some things is worse'n the joint, Fathima said.

Yes, replied Lucious, in a thick voice. Maybe.

Lucious kept his head down and Fathima watched him for a minute. Then he shook his head slowly from side to side and went back up to the front. The white man started to say something to him as he went by and then must have thought better of it and turned to the woman instead, uttering a laugh that was cut short when Fathima's head whipped around.

Lucious Exposed

A couple of minutes later the white couple left, laughing, the man's arm around the woman's waist. Soon after that, Fathima came walking, white towel in hand, making his rounds. Stopping in front of Lucious, he looked down at the man and said, You want another drink?

Lucious just stared ahead at the pool table, at the balls caroming. The balls stopped moving, but the man who had the next shot waited. Everyone was watching Lucious.

No thank you, he said. He didn't look at Fathima, or at anyone else, just kept staring at the pool table.

Well, man, you got to buy a drink here or you got to git. Don't want no loafers here.

Lucious seemed to consider that for a moment. Then he stood up and put his empty glass on one of the little wall holders behind him. He turned and faced Fathima. Surprisingly, he seemed to be about the same size as the bartender, though more muscular and not so fat. He drew his shoulders back, expanding his chest until it seemed the buttons would pop clear off and the sleeves seemed to tighten around his upper arms. His eyes were wide and there was red in the whites and for a moment the two men stood there, and a collective breath was held as everyone in the bar sensed the tension, and then it was over, and Lucious seemed to sink into the floor a little, and he said, in a small, still voice.

Well, then, I guess I'll go.

I know what you did, Fathima said as Lucious moved away, and the words seemed to strike the man in the back physically, almost like a blow. He slowed a step, hesitated, and then commenced to walk once again.

Lucious! The name was spat out with force and fury, hurled like a fireball, the sound filling every speck of space in the room.

This time Lucious stopped.

And turned.

I know what you did, Lucious. He reached into his pocket, pulled out the folded up newspaper articles and wadded them up and threw it at him. It still ain't right. You got a powerful stink about you, man. That man shit on you, Lucious.

Lucious stared at Fathima for a space that seemed to suck all the oxygen from the room, and then said, I'm not you, nigger, and he was saying it to only one person, and the way he said the word *nigger* was not hard or vicious or meanspirited but in a voice that had everything of what could be called a *human* quality. He reached down, picked up the wadded paper he'd thrown at him, turned and walked toward the front. Halfway there, he turned around as if he were about to say something else. Fathima looked up and said, Yeah? Lucious started to speak and then must have changed his mind. He put his head down and walked out the front door.

There was a split second when the only sound in the Mockingbird Café was that of Bert Parks on the TV.

And here she is. The winner. Therrrre she is, Miss Ahh— and then the hubbub started up again, balls clicking on the pool table, glasses clinking, the buzz of voices, laughter. Fathima walked up to the front and turned the TV off, twisted the knob so savagely it broke in his hand. He looked at the piece of plastic for a moment and then hurled it from him with the suddenness of a pitcher picking off a baserunner who's leaned a little too much toward second at just the wrong time.

Things Go Bad

At that instant, the front door opened and back in came Lucious.

Man— Fathima said and was cut off when Lucious held up his hand.

They comin', he said. He stepped to the side away from the door and it opened once again and in stepped two men, the first the man named Sam and right behind him a cop in uniform. Lucious stepped forward and there was a flash in his hand and the man named Sam tried to scream but couldn't as his throat was sliced from ear to ear and all that came out was a gurgle and he sank to his knees. The man behind him reached for his sidearm, fumbling with the snap and with as quick a move as Fathima had ever seen, he, too, was slumping to the floor, clutching at his throat which was spewing crimson.

Can you give me a few minutes? Lucious said to Fathima.

All Fathima could manage was a nod.

Lucious looked at him and there was a small smile on his lips. You were right, brother. There's some things worse'n the joint. Thank you for opening my eyes.

Fathima nodded again and then the man was gone.

He walked down to the other end of the bar, picked up his bar rag and began to polish a glass. There wasn't a sound in the entire bar. Fathima looked back at the boys in the back around the pool table and finally spoke. I guess I ought to call the police, he said. I just can't remember that number.

anything like that.

When he'd entered the café he'd been the only customer but, as the noon hour approached, it soon began to fill up. It was evident he was a stranger in town as about everyone who entered glanced his way, and out of the corner of his eye he could see folks at various tables glancing over his way whispering behind their hands.

It didn't much bother him. It was a small town, after all, and most likely any new face would be a subject for discussion. Which was why he didn't want to linger where he stood out so prominently. Who knows if there was a fox in the henhouse? He knew of plenty of instances where colored men served their white masters to maintain the status quo. The Civil War might be over, but old relationships die hard and often survive for decades. So, his hunger sated, it was time to move on. Before departing, he placed an order for carryout of more ribs and a container of sweet tea. Who knew when he might find another place to eat?

The second he left, he heard the rise of voices behind him, and chuckled. No doubt they were talking about him. He started walking down the street toward what looked like the edge of the town and a road leading out of there. His plan was to walk until he found a railroad track and look for a place where trains slowed down so he could jump on and continue his journey to Houston. Just before the buildings ended, a block where only a few small houses stood, beyond which was a thick woods, he was startled to hear a male voice saying, Hey! You, Tom!

He looked over to see a group of young colored men standing beside one of the houses. Half a dozen young guys, ages ranging from late teens to early twenties. Two of which he thought he recognized as being in the café who had left before he did.

He chose to ignore them and continued walking westward. None of them alone looked like they'd be much of a match for him—after all, he stood six foot six inches and was in the best shape of his life, and he had no doubt he could easily whip three or four of them with ease—but six of them posed a problem. If it came to what it looked like it was going to, his thought was to take out the biggest two quickly and hope the rest of them backed off. It looked clearly as if they meant to rob him.

He turned to face them. You boys might want to reconsider this, he said. He reached down, extracted his razor from his sock. I ain't playin', he said. Come ahead if you want, but this ain't gonna be like you thought.

He could tell that at least a couple of them were having second thoughts when he brought out his straight edge, but he could also tell they didn't want to back down in front of their friends. He marked two whose body language was easy to read and put them out of his mind. Those would stay back unless it looked like he was losing. That made the odds better. Only four to really deal with. The guy who'd spoken to him first looked like the leader. Him, he was going to take down first.

He also knew the way these things usually went down. The bigmouth leader would start jawing at him, trying to sell him a wolf ticket. That was when he was supposed to jaw back and after some of that back and forth stuff to work up his courage, the guy'd make a move.

Fuck that.

He didn't wait on him at all, but stepped forward—no, make that *ran* forward, right at the guy, a light-skinned Negro commonly referred to as a "high yella," and quicker than the guy expected, took half his nose off with his razor. The others hesitated a second and that was all he needed to swipe at the guy next to the first guy—who had bent over, moaning and grabbing for his nose. He caught him across the arm he brought up in self-defense and more blood flowed. The remaining four spread out to try and surround him but Lucious had expected that and just went after the third guy he'd identified as being one of the aggressive ones. This one surprised him by pivoting and running away as fast as he could. That left five, and two were pretty much out of commission. A second guy backed away until he was out of reach. Two left who weren't hurt already.

This was going to be easier than he thought. Except one of the remaining guys, one of those he'd initially figured to be more passive, reached into his pocket and pulled out a gun.

And shot him. The man didn't hesitate, just pulled the trigger. Hit him in the side.

At that, the rest of the little mob finally got scared. First one, then another and then the rest of them turned and ran. Including the one who'd shot him. Possibly because he acted like he hadn't even felt it and started toward him with his razor. Possibly also because he acted like the gunshot didn't bother him any more than a bee sting.

In seconds, they'd all gone. Even the two he'd cut.

It was then that he slumped to his knees. He pulled up his shirt and inspected the wound. It didn't look like much—a small wound—and he could see it had gone clear through his side. The weapon had looked like a little bitty .25 caliber. A lady's gun.

It still hurt, but not all that much. He waited, sweat pouring down his face until the moment of shock had passed, then he stood up again, picked up his bag of ribs and tea, and began walking out of town. Once he reached where the woods began, he left the road and entered the forest.

Half an hour later he sat down, slumping against an ancient oak tree. It took him awhile to get to a sitting position. The pain had begun to increase. His wound began to bleed. Not heavily, but steadily. He closed his eyes and tried to calm himself. The sun was slipping away and the evening air began to cool a bit from the sweltering and oppressive heat of the day.

Mandy Has a Secret

One of the pups, the runt of the litter, died early in the morning.

The woman looked out in the yard in the first hours of the new day, in time to see the other dogs tearing it to shreds.

You dogs git! She rushed over and swung wildly at them with the business end of her broom. Yelping as she connected, they finally scattered and stood a short distance away, growling softly and watching the woman out of the corners of yellow eyes. The woman snatched up the mangled pup and carried it back to the house. One of the dogs, the male pit bull, made a run at her back, nipping her heel and drawing blood as she opened the door.

Inside, she bandaged up the slight wound with a rag and stripped the remaining flesh off the dog's bones and dropped it into a pot. She poured four inches of water in the bottom, and put the pot on the stove. When it was done, she took it from the fire and placed the meat, bones and all, on a tin plate and placed it on the table. The water she poured into five tin cups. There were about four swallows of broth in each.

Get up, get up, she said, moving from child to child on their pallets. Food. The smell of the dog meat nauseated her and she had to sit down for a minute. Then, she took a tiny sliver of the meat she had set aside and forced herself to chew and swallow it. The taste made her lightheaded. She picked up the baby and went out to the porch to sit down. The baby fussed until she set her down to crawl on the ground.

The rest of her brood came straggling out, some to sit hunkered down on the porch beside her and one or two of the others scattered out in the yard, heads down, kicking at rocks, making marks in the dust with twigs. Before long, the dogs began circling the baby, who had made her way out into the yard, nipping at her body, the same way they had the puppy's.

Stop it! Stop it, stop it, stop! Amelia screamed, running at the pack, apron flapping, arms windmilling. The dogs skulked away, tongues lolling in their mouths, their eyes yellow and unblinking. Snatching up her baby on the run, she cradled her in her arms, screaming at the other children to get inside. Breathlessly, she slammed the door behind them. Crystal was, miraculously, mostly unharmed, except for one arm oozing blood from half a dozen teeth marks, thankfully none of them deep. She cleansed the wounds with spittle and wiped them with the hem of her skirt.

Mama, I'm hungry.

Mama, my head hurts. My tummy, too.

Mama, what's the matter with Daddy's dogs?

Mandy, alone, kept quiet. Finally, she spoke up. I hope he never comes back.

Amelia was visibly shocked. What? Why would you say that, Mandy?

Mandy's eyes grew big. She was visibly frightened of what she'd said. She sat there, silent for a moment, and then seemed to gather up her courage. Because, Mama… she hesitated and then plunged ahead. Sometimes he … does things.

Amelia nearly fainted at the words. She motioned to her to come back with her into her bedroom, pulling the burlap bags that served as a curtain behind them and indicated to Mandy that she sit on the bed. She took the chair in the corner. She forced herself to hold up her head and look her oldest daughter in the eye. What do you mean, child? She had to ask the question, even though the possible answer frightened her to death.

Mandy held her stare for a long moment, then tossed her curls defiantly. You know what I mean, Mama. When he gets drunk and you're asleep. He

… touches me. He's done more than that. Once. I told him I'd kill him if he ever did that again. He just laughed, said if there was any killing, it'd be him killing me and you, too, if I told. Mama … he … he did it *here.* He said it would keep me a virgin, else no boy would have me. She couldn't bring herself to make it any clearer, just kind of lifted up her bottom, looking away from her mother when she did.

Amelia's face drained of all blood. She stood up abruptly and crossed the room to her daughter and wrapped her arms around her. Oh, Mandy! Both began to weep, great wrenching sobs from both. Amelia was the first to gain control of herself. She leaned back, her hand combing Mandy's hair back from her face. Never again, baby. Never again. You have my word. That man … will never step foot in this home again. I promise you.

Oh, Mama! Mandy unleashed another series of sobbing, loud and shrill and full of pain. Gradually, she got herself under control, and hugged her mother and stood up. Mama. I was just so scared to say… Amelia put her hand over her daughter's mouth. Quiet, Mandy. Hush, child. It's going to be okay.

They kept inside the next two days, during which Amelia and Mandy held several conversations. She didn't say anything to her daughter, but she'd already made a vow to kill her husband.

It was time to tell her. Mandy, she said, Arnold knows you're not his birth daughter.

He does?

He pretends he doesn't, but he knows. I think he knew the minute you were born, when he saw your red hair, but if he didn't know for sure then, he knew by the time you were ten. The more baby fat you lost, the more you looked like Billy. Anyone would have to be blind not to know who your real daddy was.

Why didn't you leave him? Why didn't you go and live with Billy?

She struggled for the words.

Because we were married, she said at last. It's for better or for worse. It's not just some words. It's a sacred vow.

Because we were married, she repeated, her eyes widening as she realized she had put her daughter at risk with her husband for a reason that now seemed utterly foolish and maybe even insane.

Oh God, she said. What have I done? She crumbled to her knees. I'm so sorry, Mandy, she said.

Mama.

Mandy took her mother's face in her hands and forced her to look up at her.

Mama, don't blame yourself. You never had a chance. I know that. Please don't blame yourself. I couldn't stand that. She paused. But now you've changed. I can see that, plain as day. That … *man* … will never do anything else to us. Never again.

Amelia tried to say something but tears blinded her eyes and the words choked in her throat.

Shh, Mama. It's okay.

Why's Mama crying? It was Mary. She and Abby had come up to stand beside them. Abby's hand in her older sister's.

It's all right, children, Amelia said, wiping her tears away with her apron and standing up. I'm just tired. I think I'll just lie down for a bit.

Crystal

Outside, the dogs, always waiting there, even at night. Why don't they go away? Amelia thought. She watched the dogs circle the bitch and her litter early on the third morning before the kids awoke. Once the first puppy was attacked and killed, the bitch joined the others in ripping the flesh off her own offspring and choking it down. When they awoke, she took the children to the back of the cabin in their bedroom and tried to get them to sing a song, so they couldn't watch or hear. The morning sun toasted the cabin even more, bringing with it nothing but heat and suffocating air.

Arnold wouldn't be coming back. She was certain of that. She had mixed feelings about that. Glad on the one hand, and a gnawing feeling of being cheated out of her vengeance on the other. The blood thirst ran high in her.

Everything outside was brown and red, and even if there had been some weeds to dig up or pick, the dogs wouldn't let them out. They guarded the house, waiting, making it crazy to even think about opening the door. She had tried to go for water from the creek if it wasn't completely dried up and they were ready for her, one hurling his body at the door as she started to open it, clawing at the screen, teeth tearing at the wooden frame.

Well, she thought. So.

If there was a God… She nearly gasped aloud when that thought first presented itself, but the more it appeared, the more she began to get used to the possibility that she and her children were completely on their own. It was the first time in her life she'd even considered such a thing, and in one way it was very frightening and in another, oddly liberating.

The water was down to a tepid six inches in the bucket. She had been rationing it for days, allowing only tiny sips for the children, one small sip a day for herself. Finally, she began moistening a bit of a rag and letting them suck on it. It was odd—the longer they went without food and water, the less they seemed to want either. She supposed it was just the body's way of survival. She was experiencing the same lack of hunger and thirst.

The baby's lips became chapped and then cracked. Then she quit drinking and Amelia was reduced to moistening her lips with a bit of a rag. Her little ribs showed clearly and then she got an infection Amelia couldn't understand. Her skin turned red and her tummy began to swell and that seemed impossible. There was nothing Amelia could think of to do to relieve her misery. She cried constantly, a thin, reedy wail, and Amelia and Mandy took turns holding her close and rocking her. To little avail.

And then, the crying ceased. There was a series of little hiccups and then nothing. At first, Amelia was overjoyed. She thought the tide had turned. It hadn't. She'd simply stopped breathing. All the tension left Crystal's tiny body and she became a limp doll. Her blue eyes remained open and Amelia had a strangely comforting thought—that she was looking toward a better tomorrow. She leaned over and kissed her lips and all thought fled her mind for a brief time. Once again, just like other bleak times in her life, she didn't give in to tears, although she came close.

When the baby died, Mandy quit talking. Let's sing a song, Amelia said. *Rock of Ages*—it's your favorite, but Mandy just sat in the corner, sucking her thumb. She hadn't ever sucked her thumb when she was a baby, but she did so now. Amelia bundled the baby in a blanket and put her in the pie safe. The other children seemed not to notice. They barely looked up from the various places on the floor where they lay, their eyes half-lidded or closed.

And then, from out of nowhere, blinding tears came for the first time since she was a child. For a full ten minutes she sat on a kitchen chair, the floodgates open and tears flowed without cessation down her cheeks. At last she stopped, sniffed once, hard, and got up and walked to the front window and looked out, trying to figure out a solution to their plight. Nothing came to her.

The sound of the dogs was very clear now, as they lolled on their haunches by the porch, sending up anemic wolf-like howls, as if they were waiting for an answer from inside the cabin. There was no response to be had. They had never howled like this before and Amelia couldn't understand why they were agitated and then it dawned on her. They were acknowledging, maybe even honoring … Crystal's death.

She went back to her chair and put her head in her hands and began to weep again. It was all too much. Her baby dead, the rest of her family prisoners in their own home starving and dying of dehydration. She knew, as much as she'd ever known anything in her life, that Arnold wasn't coming back. She'd be relieved at that if it didn't mean their death sentences.

She lay down her head on the table. Then, she felt something on her back. Mandy's hand, patting her like she was the child.

Mama, what are we going to do?

She had no answer. She lifted her head. Mandy sat down in the chair next to her and looked at her, expectation in her eyes that her mother would come up with a solution to their plight. Amelia just shook her head.

Mama. Amelia nearly jumped at the voice. It was James who'd come up behind her.

What, son?

Mama, it's the dogs won't let us out isn't it? It wasn't a question, but she answered as if it was.

Yes, James. It's the dogs.

I can get them back into the pens.

Oh, James! She was suddenly frightened. Nobody can get them into the pens. I don't think even your daddy can now.

He stood there, his chin quivering and his eyes bright. I can, Mama. I know I can. They like me.

That was true. The dogs adored James. He was the one who fed them when Arnold was gone, who played with them, tossing them sticks to retrieve, petted them constantly. Maybe…

But she couldn't allow it. The dogs were different now. They'd gone feral and once that happened there was no going back. They were starving, and all humans meant to them now was food.

I'm goin', Mama.

She stood up quickly to stop him but he was already out of her reach. By the door, he reached into the box of kindling and grabbed a stout piece of wood and was out the door, closing it behind him. The instant before he closed the door, she heard the dogs cease their howling.

No! she screamed but he was already gone.

She ran to where she kept her machete and ran for the door. Mandy followed, grabbing her own stick from the wood box.

Shot

Sometime around midnight Lucious awakened, his body stiff and sore, his side hurting mightily. Although it had been a small caliber handgun and the wound was only a flesh wound, he thought it might be infected and that concerned him. A night in a hospital would probably fix him right up, but he didn't dare risk going to any medical facility. He wished he was back in Detroit or even in New Orleans—he knew where to go to get help there, but out here he was totally in the open, completely vulnerable. Even more so since he was a black man. He didn't know if they'd figured out who he was back in New Orleans, but a check of his fingerprints might turn up the paper on him from Detroit.

No, he was screwed.

And feverish.

He moaned and forced himself to stand. For a second he wavered, his legs trembling, then he found purchase and stood without falling. He took a step forward and then another. A few feet from the tree he saw a thick branch forked at one end on the ground and picked it up, using it for a cane. He began moving further into the woods, leaning on his makeshift crutch.

After an hour of this he sat down beside a large tree and opened the bag with the ribs he'd bought back in town. He ate about a fourth of them, rationing the rest for later. Who knew when he'd find his next meal?

He felt better. Enough to continue hiking through the woods.

Twenty minutes later, he stopped dead in his tracks.

Noises behind him.

Voices.

He slid down a small gully, holding back the yelp of pain at the fire reignited in his side. It was about three feet to the bottom of the ditch and it was filled with leaves. A large log was there and he scrambled to it and began grabbing handfuls of leaves to build a mound, and when he had enough, he scooched underneath it and reached out to cover himself with leaves and twigs.

None too soon. Almost the instant he finished covering himself, the source of the voices stood just above him on the edge of the gully. It was obvious they didn't see him.

Yet.

Willie, fuck this, man. He's long gone.

Shut up, Manfred. I *know* he's in here. He's hurt, man. He can't get far.

Shit. A third voice. Three of the young men from yesterday. Y'all don't even know if he's got any money.

You a fool, said the first voice. Lucious recognized it as the man whose nose he'd cut. Lucile said he had a wad would choke a horse when he paid.

One of the other two men laughed. *Lucile* got a wad would choke a horse.

There was some laughter over that and then some whispering and muted voices, and then he heard them moving away. They got further and further from him and then it grew quiet again. He waited another ten minutes to be sure they were gone then sat up, shaking the leaves off his shoulders.

Well, looky here. The man whose nose he'd nearly cut off stepped out from behind a tree. Hey! C'mon back. Here he is, like I said, he yelled. He grinned and pulled out a gun from his trousers pocket.

Lucious put his hands in the air, heard the other two men come crashing back through the dry undergrowth.

You fixin' to rob a black man, son?

The man took a step closer to him on the edge of the gully.

I ain't your son, old man. And, seems to me black folks' money spends same as white folks. Throw up that straight razor. Now.

Lucious reached down and plucked out his razor from his sock. He held it in his hand for a long second as if he was debating whether or not to charge the man and his companions and wreak more damage on them, but reconsidered and ended up tossing the razor up where it fell to the ground beside their leader.

Now, throw up your money.

Lucious reached into his pocket and took out a handful of bills. He crumpled them into a wad and threw it at the man, who reached down and plucked it from the ground.

This is it? Sixteen dollars?

Yeah. Big score for a little man. They call you Jesse James?

Jesse James this, old man. He pointed the gun at Lucious, pulled the trigger twice in quick succession.

James and the Dogs

James was down. As Amelia and then Mandy flew out the door, all they saw was a churning mass of dogs and an arm that stuck up for a second and then disappeared again into the boil of snarling, growling, moiling canines.

James! Amelia screamed, and waded into the fray, wielding her machete right and left as she struck one dog and then another, eliciting yelps with each blow. Behind her, Mandy swung her own club, lifting one of the black and tans several feet into the air.

Between the two of them, they cleared a path to James, who lay bestilled and in a silent heap, his shirt ripped off, blood covering every inch of his torso. Amelia reached down with her free hand and tried to grab him under his arm, her grasp slipping on the gore. Mandy came up and bent down herself to reach beneath his other arm and together they managed to gain hold of him and begin to drag him toward the cabin, striking out as best they could at the snarling pack that had regrouped to an extent and began circling them, jaws snapping, blood-thirsty howls erupting. Somehow they managed to get him to the porch and up onto it with only a severe bite to Mandy's leg, and Amelia got the door open and they pulled James inside and slammed it shut behind them.

Between the two of them, they hoisted James up onto the table. He appeared to be breathing, but barely, with short, shallow pants, his chest rising and falling. His features were indistinguishable, blood covering not only his face but his entire chest and legs where his trousers were torn and ripped. What made Amelia more frightened than anything was that his breathing was the only sound he emitted. It was as if his pain had taken the power of vocalization away completely.

And then she saw why. Wiping away the gore from his face with the hem of her dress, she saw the worst wound. A significant hole in his throat, from which bubbled blood with each exhalation. Ferociously, she ripped her dress and took the cloth and balled it up in her fist and jammed it into the hole. It seemed to help.

Oh, Sugarman, she whispered. My precious little Sugarman.

Mandy slumped into a chair and began sobbing loudly. Her little sister Abby came out of the bedroom and walked over to her and began patting her on her back. Abby seemed not to notice James lying on the table. Amelia picked him up in her arms, walked to the children's bedroom and placed him on his pallet. She picked up the comforter on her own bed and came back and placed it over her son. He was breathing regularly now.

She knew what she had to do. She fetched her sewing basket and threaded a needle with white thread. James stirred several times, but thankfully didn't waken until she'd finished sewing the hole in his throat shut. He seemed to breathe better once she was done.

She went to the kitchen and sat down in a chair opposite Mandy.

Is he … okay? Mandy said.

Yes. But he needs a doctor.

Those dogs … I hate those dogs. I want to kill every single one of them.

I know.

Mandy lifted her head and stared hard at her mother. I want to kill Daddy, too, she said.

Amelia just sighed. I know, child. I know.

Abby walked around the table to her mother. What's wrong with James, Mama? Is he sleeping?

She reached out and drew Abby to her. Yes, child. He's very tired. Let's just let him sleep.

running from it.

She ripped her dress and took the scrap and wrapped it tightly around her daughter's leg. And began praying, beseeching a God who remained silent.

Minutes later, she checked the wound. It was still seeping blood but much more slowly. She wanted to get her into bed but didn't have the strength, so she brought one of the children's pallets into the kitchen and rolled Mandy onto it and covered her with a quilt.

Sentencing

Thirty days, the judge said. Next case.

Just like that, Arnold Critchin's domicile for the next month was settled.

You sunuvabitch! Arnold ran toward the judge's bench and got to within five feet of it before a deputy grabbed him from behind by his shirt and spun him down on his knees. In an instant, another deputy was on him and pinned him to the floor. The judge—Judge Crenshaw—was already on his feet, a big ol' Navy Colt .45 in his hand, drawn from beneath his robe.

Get that piece of shit out of my courtroom! he thundered. And, that'll be another thirty days.

The deputies had to cuff both his hands as well as put a chain on his feet so all he could do was scuffle along behind them, cussing with every step, yelling at the judge what he was going to do if he ever caught him outside his courtroom, on his way out the door.

When they got back to the jail, Billy asked them how long Critchin was going to be their guest.

You ain't gonna like this, Billy, said George.

He didn't.

Christ! he said. Just take him out back and shoot him, will'ya? I can't stand to have to see that asshole for two months. He's only been here a couple of weeks and it seems like half my life. Just bury him deep. Foster, the younger of the two deputies, looked at his partner, who laughed and said, Forget it, Foster. He ain't serious. A second later, he looked over at Billy behind his desk. Are you?

For way of an answer, Billy just snorted and went back to work on his paperwork.

A few minutes later, he looked up and said, Is Faustus back yet?

Told he wasn't, he sighed. Well, somebody's got to go out to see about Critchin's wife and kids.

George looked at him and shook his head. Sheriff, we got nobody. Dewey's out sick and we need everybody else at work.

Billy mumbled something under his breath, sounded like *shit* and slapped on his hat. I'm going over to Roy's. We gotta do something about his family. Maybe I can find someone to deputize over there who isn't too drunk.

He tried not to worry, but he knew how little Arnold cared about his family. His dogs were far more important to the man.

Deputizing a Couple of Volunteers

He walked into Roy's Tap and looked around to see who was there. Maybe nine, ten guys and a couple of women. The usual hardcore drunks always there in the mornings, early afternoons. He almost walked back out to look somewhere else for someone to deputize and then realized that all they had to do was ride out to Amelia's place and check on her and the kids. Even a drunk could do that.

He walked back to a table near the rear where the biggest group sat. Half a dozen men, all of whom he knew. Most of whom he'd arrested at one time or another. For little, piddly stuff mostly—drunk driving, bar fights, the usual.

Hi Teddy. Boys, he said, nodding.

Hey, Billy. Have a seat. The man he'd spoken to reached over and pulled out a chair for him. Want a beer?

No thanks, he said. I'm on duty. I'm kind of here on official business. I need a couple of guys to deputize, do a particular job.

Teddy said, Hell, I'm available. You need someone to bust down some doors? He laughed as did the rest of them.

Billy smiled. Nope. Nothing that much fun. I need two guys to take a little trip up the road. Check in on Arnold Critchin's family, see how they're doing. Pays fifteen dollars and a meal.

Hell, for that kind of money, I'm in. This from Merle Swanson, a part-

The Man in the Dream

It was dusk before Lucious regained consciousness. For a moment, he was completely confused as to where he was and then it began coming back to him. He didn't move at first. He didn't know if the men who'd robbed and shot him were still there. When he heard the chittering of squirrels, he knew he was alone.

And hurt bad.

Both shots by the man named Willie had found his body. Another shot in the gut and this one hadn't passed through but was lodged there, somewhere. And the other bullet struck his head. He could feel the pounding before his fingers found where it had hit him and at first he thought it might have been a fatal shot and he was in the final stage before he died, but as much as it hurt, he felt the furrow the bullet had made and knew it had only grazed him. Probably the reason he'd become unconscious. Maybe what had saved his life. The robbers had probably seen the blood and figured he was gone.

He groaned and managed to sit up.

He wasn't dead yet but he knew that if he didn't get help soon he would be. It took nearly ten minutes, but he eventually made it to the top of the ravine where he found his razor. He didn't think he could bend over enough to stick it back in his sock, so he just dropped it into his pocket.

He began walking as best he could, using the same stick he'd used before, finding it where he'd dropped it. All he could think of was he needed to find a human being. Someone who could help him. He knew if he ended up in a hospital the odds were good it would be discovered who he was and he'd be sent back to Michigan. Or maybe Louisiana. He had no idea if a warrant was out on him for what he'd done to the two cops in New Orleans. It didn't much matter where they'd end up sending him. It was all jail. But at least he'd be alive.

He'd go as far as he could and if that wasn't far enough, then so be it.

It was almost totally dark and he'd barely gone a quarter of a mile. He was about to find a tree to prop himself against and try to get some sleep when he noticed a break in the trees just ahead. Groaning, he forced himself to stumble the hundred yards to it and was glad he did.

It was a road. Truth, it wasn't much of a road, more of a dirt path but wide enough that a car or truck could travel on it.

He began lurching forward on it. The only goal he had was to keep walking as far as he could and hope that it led to somebody who could help him. He wasn't optimistic but it was all he had.

The trees began to thin out and he saw he was among farmland. Poor farmland, but at least it showed the hand of human endeavor in the rows of scraggly brown cornstalks. If there was a field, there'd be a house somewhere. The heat since he'd left the forest was overwhelming, even in the nighttime.

He kept on, his mind blank, his only aim to keep putting one foot down and then the other. The holes in his gut were screaming and he tried his best to ignore it.

One more step … just one more step … just one more…

Then he saw it. Just off the road. A cabin. If a flash of dry lightning hadn't flared just then and briefly illuminated it, he would have passed by.

His stomach was on absolute fire.

He kept going through the dry dust that was between him and the cabin. He'd almost reached the cabin when he heard them. All around him.

Dogs.

Snarling, angry dogs. One of them, a pit bull, lunged at him and it was all he could do to strike at him with his crutch. Luckily, the blow landed, the dog yelped and the rest of them backed off a step. He tried to yell to alert the house but all he could manage was a weak croak, and that must have signaled to the dogs his vulnerability as they began to close on him, their jaws open and snarling and dripping with saliva. He struck out once again and fell to the ground as his balance fled him. Dogs, mostly hounds, all over him, biting and growling and snapping… He knew he was done. His last thought was of his little girl, lying in a hospital bed on a dialysis machine. He continued to thrash against the attacking dogs but his mind was elsewhere and then everything went dark.

It seemed like hours before he came to, briefly. He had a quick image of a tall, lanky woman and a young girl with fiery red hair forcing him to his feet, a dog yelping as the woman struck at it with something in her hand—a knife?—and then blessed darkness again.

The Black Man in the Dream

The dogs woke her.

Odd, they weren't on the porch or even in the yard, but further out, near the road. She knew she shouldn't, but she had to see. She stepped out onto the porch, machete in hand. Behind her something rustled and she glanced back to see Mandy standing up, the quilt she'd put on around her shoulders.

What is it, Mama?

Mandy!

She ran to her. You can't be up, girl! Your leg…

I'm better, Mama. I feel okay. I just needed some rest. What's that noise?

She put her finger to her lips and motioned her to come forward to stand by her.

I don't know. It looks like the dogs have hold of something. An animal or something. It's big, like a cow. Or maybe a bear? It's big, whatever it is.

Mandy took a step forward and peered into the dark beyond the open door. Involuntarily, she shrank back. In the light from the half-moon, Amelia saw her face and the terror on it.

Mama, it's a man!

Lordy! She wasn't sure what to do. The dogs could kill her if she went to his aid. On the other hand… She made a decision. Mandy, stay in the house.

She didn't wait to see if her daughter did as she'd ordered but went through the door, stepped off the porch and began to walk toward the roiling dogs. She hadn't taken but a couple of steps before she realized Mandy had disobeyed her and was just behind her, with a large stick of kindling in her hands. Mandy— she started to say something else but the dogs were louder and she could hear their jaws snapping and weak moans coming from the man. C'mon then, but be careful.

The two women began running at the pack and screaming at them.

The dogs were so busy with the prey on the ground that they failed to hear the two come up behind them until the machete flashed and one of the black-and-tans yelped in pain from a blow across his back. He whined and crept away, tail between his legs. Another hound took a blow from Mandy's club and slunk away as well. The rest stood their ground, the male pit bull, the alpha leader, refused to give ground, even creeping nearer the two women. Mandy split away from her mother and began toward the downed man, swinging the stick as hard as she could, striking dogs right and left. For an instant, Amelia stood watching in amazement and then regained control of herself and went after the pit bull with her weapon, swinging it like a Viking clearing Celts in a pitched battle, severing one of its ears. He didn't yelp, but he did back off.

Reaching the man, both she and Mandy reached down to grab an arm and for an instant the man regained consciousness, and he opened his eyes. They'd barely taken a step when Amelia really saw his face and screamed.

It was the huge black man from her dream.

The Boogey Man

After that, it was all a blur. She thought that Mandy had screamed to help her and she thought she was going to faint, but somehow she got herself back under some sort of control and between the two of them, they managed to get him up the porch and into the house, the dogs nipping at their heels and snarling just beyond reach of their weapons. They wouldn't have succeeded if the man hadn't regained semi-consciousness and helped them as much as he was able to, stumbling forward under their arms, a fire in his gut and a fever on his brow and unable to focus on anything other than struggling to put one foot in front of the other. The second they made the house he slipped into unconsciousness and it wasn't until two days passed that he came to again and saw that he was lying in a bed and there were children standing around, staring at him. Two small girls and a teenaged girl.

Mama, he's awake!

Mama, he's a colored man!

Mama, Daddy don't allow colored men in the house.

Mama, is he the Boogey Man?

Another voice, from someone he couldn't see without twisting his neck and he couldn't do that without considerable pain, said, Hush, children. This man isn't the Boogey Man. He's just hurt and needs our help. Go play and leave him alone.

She appeared in his vision when she walked around the bed.

You're in bad shape, she said to him. Somebody shot you. She reached behind her and drew up a chair and sat down where he could see her. You in trouble with the law?

Despite himself, he managed a weak smile. Ma'am, I'm in trouble with everyone.

You want to tell me about it?

No, ma'am. I don't.

I knew you were coming, she said. He didn't speak, just waited to see if she would explain her statement.

I've been seeing you, she went on. In my dreams.

Your dreams?

She seemed to stifle a smile. More like nightmares. She paused. For the thing which I greatly feared is come upon me, and that which I was afraid of is come unto me.

Before he could respond, she added. I think I was wrong. I think you came here for another reason. Maybe to save us.

He said, I'm not sure I can do that. I'm in pretty bad shape. I can't even save myself. As if to emphasize his point, he coughed and then grimaced. She moved behind him and adjusted his pillow so that it would support his head.

That thing you said, he said, was a verse from Job in the Bible, wasn't it?

Yes, she said. Job 3:25.

I thought so. I hope I'm not a bad thing come into your life. I don't mean to be.

They were both quiet for a moment.

You had a bad infection, she said. With the older wound. It's cleared up now. I'm afraid the second one is bad. The bullet's still in there.

How'd you get the infection to go down?

She gave him a small smile. With slippery elm bark and flax seed. It's something my mother taught me. She hesitated. And with maggots.

He started and then coughed.

Maggots?

Yes, she said. You had a bad infection. They cleaned it up.

Maggots?

They only eat the bad flesh.

Oh, God! He looked as if he was going to start crying.

Amelia laughed. You city folks!

He started to say something else and then his eyes rolled back in his head and he passed out. She put her hand to his forehead and snatched it back. He was burning up.

Mama. It was Mandy.

What, child?

It's the dogs. Most of 'em are up on the porch.

She got up and went into the other room and looked out the window. Mandy was right. It was clear they weren't going to get out.

Her baby girl dead, the others maybe only a day or even less before they succumbed. And now, a man lying near death in her bed. Overpowering everything were the odors. The decomposing body of her baby, the stench of feces and urine from the pot they were all forced to use with the outhouse yards away in distance but miles away in accessibility, the body odors of too many people in too small of a space.

Only Mandy seemed to have any strength left at all and that wasn't much. Her daughter's eyes were sunken, her cheeks pallid and wan, her hands trembling. So far her bite wound wasn't infected, but if she didn't get her to a doctor soon chances were good it might be, no matter how she treated it. The other two were sleeping—more like unconscious. She could see the black man lying in bed, asleep or unconscious, his face beaded in sweat. She could hear him panting in short breaths from the kitchen. The only thing she could hold onto was that if somehow they could live through just one more day, then help might arrive. It wasn't much of a hope, but it was all she had. Survive for one more day…

They needed food. It was their only hope. Just a little. Enough to sustain life for one more day and hope…

An idea began to form. At first she tried to dismiss it, think about something else, but it kept niggling at her.

Help Is on the Way

Halfway to the Critchin place, the squad car's engine began to smoke and a loud, knocking noise emanated from the engine.

Peering in at the engine, Faustus said, It's a rod. Fucking thing threw a rod.

I know that, Eugene said. Smiley at the garage said it was okay.

Faustus slammed the hood back down. Well, obviously Smiley don't know shit.

The two men looked at each other, then down the road in the direction of the Critchin place, then back at each other.

What now? Eugene said.

Hell if I know. It's eight miles there or eight miles back. Whaddya think? Go on to the Critchin's?

And carry all these groceries? If they're in trouble how we gonna do anything with no car?

Yeah. Eugene removed his hat, scratched his head. Go back to town? It's eight, nine miles. And, it's hot.

Faustus sighed. It's gonna be hotter when we get there. Billy's gonna be smokin'. He started walking back toward town.

What about the food and stuff?

Carry 'em if you want. Not me. I'm susceptible to heat stroke.

Eugene looked at the back seat where the bags were, hesitated a minute, then turned and walked fast to catch up with his partner.

Billy's gonna be smokin', he said.

Tell me something I don't know. C'mon. Pick it up, Eugene. It's gonna get hotter.

Escape

Rather than wait for Bear and Teddy to show up at his office, Billy decided to walk over to Roy's Tap to see if he could head them off. If they were there, he'd buy them a couple rounds of beer and that'd mollify them. He hoped.

He was in luck. They were both sitting at the bar.

Hi boys, he said, swinging a leg up and over the stool to sit beside Bear.

Hey, Sheriff. We was just on our way over.

I figured. I've got some bad news for you.

He saw the looks both men gave him and quickly said to Roy, Set 'em up, Roy. Drinks on me. The scowls disappeared.

Boys, I'm sorry. My deputies just came back. Roy, give 'em another one when they're done with this one.

The two men took it better than he'd hoped.

Aw, it's okay, Billy, Teddy said.

Yeah, chimed in Bear. It's too damn hot to work today anyway.

Billy grinned, slapped down a five-dollar bill on the bar. Thanks, fellas. Appreciate your understanding. Roy? This is for these guys until it runs out.

He got off the stool and headed for the door when all of a sudden it blew open and his youngest and newest deputy, Dooley Jones, burst in.

Sheriff! Critchin's escaped!

That got everybody in the bar's attention.

Breathlessly, Dooley spewed out his tale. He was just coming in to work to relieve Lenny Barclay the night turnkey, when Arnold Critchin burst out the door, pointed a gun at him and fired. He hit the ground and by the time he collected his wits about him Critchin had disappeared. Inside, he found Lenny on the floor, holding his side to stanch the blood flowing from it. He'd shot him. An ambulance was on the way, Dooley said, and just as he said it they all heard the siren.

I think he's going to be okay, Dooley said. Looked like a flesh wound, mostly.

C'mon, Billy said to Bear and Teddy. You're deputized.

Both men looked at the beers in front of them and picked up the mugs, downing them.

We're with you, Billy, Bear said.

The four men ran to the sheriff's office, where the door stood wide open and the ambulance crew was loading Lenny into it. It was Critchin, he said to Billy. He grabbed my gun when I took him breakfast. He took that bottle you keep in the desk, too. I'm sorry, Billy.

It's okay, Lenny, Billy said. We'll get him. I know where he's going. He nodded to the ambulance attendants. You just go get fixed up.

He went into the office, followed by the three men. A quick glance told him everything. He walked over and unlocked the gun cabinet, and began handing out rifles to Bear and Teddy.

Dooley, you stay here. Call everyone, get 'em in here. All the auxiliary guys, too. Call the state police, tell 'em what happened and where we're at.

Where you're at? Where's that, Billy?

At Critchin's place. It's where he's headed.

He grabbed a rifle himself.

Let's go, boys, he said.

Arnold Meets the Deputies

I got to sit down, Faustus, Eugene said. He walked over to a log and sat down heavily on it. It's just too damned hot.

Okay, said his partner. Five minutes. We're halfway home.

Faustus walked over to sit beside Eugene, when Eugene fell backward and off the log. Faustus turned at the crack of the gun and it fired again, hitting him in the shoulder and dropping him on the spot. Lying there in a daze, he looked up and there stood Arnold Critchin holding a revolver on him. He recognized it as police issue.

Give me your gun, Arnold said.

Fuck you, Critchin, he said, reaching down to fumble at his sidearm with his injured arm. He wasn't quick enough and even if he had been he wouldn't have been able to grab the gun or fire it. The second shot hit him high on the hip and he slipped into a bottomless void.

Arnold Critchin moved to him, bent down and took out his revolver and then walked over to Eugene's body and took his as well along with his ammunition belt.

See ya in hell, assholes, he said, and began walking down the road in the direction the deputies had just come from.

Toward his cabin and his dogs. And his wife and kids.

Once he got home, everything would be all right.

He had a plan. He'd get his dogs and head for the Big Thicket. No way they'd ever be able to find him there. He might even take Mandy with him.

He stopped for a few seconds to take a long drink of whiskey from the bottle he'd liberated from the sheriff, recapped it and began walking again.

A Gruesome Discovery

They almost passed by the bodies alongside the road.

Sheriff!

Billy looked back over his shoulder at Teddy in the back seat.

Stop, Sheriff!

What is it?

Back there. He inclined his shoulder toward the way they'd come.

Billy sighed and backed up the car.

Jesus!

All three men were out of the car in a trice. Billy ran to the two downed men.

They dead? That was Bear.

I don't know, Billy said. Maybe … and then there was a low moan from Faustus.

No! Faustus is alive. Eugene's … gone.

We got to get him to the hospital, Bear said.

But, Arnold… Billy stopped. Bear was right. They had to get Faustus medical help or he'd die too.

Help me, he said. They loaded both men into the back of the car, Eugene on the floor and Faustus on the seat.

Billy made a hard decision. Teddy, you drive. Bear, you get in back with Faustus, hold this against his hip. He tore off his shirt, handed it to the man.

Get going. Get this man to the hospital and then send everybody on the force to Critchin's. Everybody. You boys, too.

Billy, you want us—

Yes! I can get to the Critchin's in an hour maybe. I might be able to save them. If I go back, it'll be too late. Now go! Drive like hell! He reached in, grabbed his rifle.

Bear looked at him, then nodded. Okay, Billy. We got it. We'll get the guys on their way.

Teddy whipped the car around.

Wait! It was Bear. Billy had already started walking away. Billy!

He turned around. What?

Your deputies don't have their guns. Neither one of 'em.

Billy nodded, grim-faced. This is gonna be a bloodbath. Get your asses going.

The car pulled away, the siren blasting, lights flashing. Billy was already going forward at a dead run. He didn't know how big of a head start Arnold had, but he was going to do his best to catch him before he got to his cabin.

Desperate Times

Ma, the children begged. Abby and Mary. Mama, I'm hungry. Fix us something to eat, please, Ma. She looked helplessly around the cabin. Mandy was asleep. The black man in her bed was asleep or unconscious. Or... A ringing began in her ears and then she realized another day had passed and they weren't whining at her. She tried to remember when she heard them last ask for food and thought it was the previous day.

Roots, she thought. Maybe somewhere out there in the dust she could find some roots. She had to try. She had to get something to eat for them. She staggered to the door on jellied legs and opened it a crack. The dogs ran up on the porch. She pushed it closed just as a hound's body slammed against it.

Get into bed, she ordered the two little girls, lost for any other course of action. Try to sleep. It'll take your minds off your stomachs.

The rest of that day and through the night the children kept waking up, calling her name. Mandy just kept sleeping and so did the man in her bed. Once, she went in and put her hand on Mandy's brow and pulled back in a rush. She dipped a rag into the precious remaining water and wiped her forehead. It seemed to help at first, but an hour later when she checked on her, she felt cold, and after that she didn't feel her again. She didn't go near the colored man, but saw his chest heaving in short, shallow breaths, his face bathed in sweat.

It was then she became aware of the smell. It must have been there all along, but this was the first she was consciously aware of it. And, she knew what it was. It was coming from both the pie safe and from the form of her son lying on the corner in the bedroom. *Oh, God.*

She went to the trunk her mother had given her, over in the far corner. From it, she took two large quilts. One, she took out to the pie safe and draped it over it. The odor seemed to lessen some. The other, she took over to where James lay, covered by a blanket. She draped the quilt over his form and tucked it in all around. There. The smell all but disappeared. In fact, it may have disappeared entirely, but she still smelled it and it was all she could do to keep from gagging. And weeping.

She kept avoiding the thought that kept coming up. It was just too horrible to contemplate. She tried to come up with something else she might do, *anything* else she might do, but one by one they all fell aside as unworkable, impossible.

There was a hole in her own stomach, and she felt something strange on her face. When she touched it with her fingers a door opened, a memory came floating up. The same wetness on her cheek. She thought back to that day when Miss Wexler called her name, had her come stand before the class, and said those things about her. Best math student I've ever had. Nice things. And the way she handed her a piece of paper as if she were presenting a queen's gift to her devoted subject. Her name was on it, and a gold seal, raised and shiny. As she made her way back to her seat, heart thumping, Miss Wexler got a laugh out of the whole class, when she said, Arnold, if you paid attention like Amelia, perhaps that glorious day will arrive when you'll finally master the multiplication tables and find yourself in the fourth grade.

Six times six, she said aloud, surprised at herself. Thirty-six. She pulled her chair up and stared out the window. The dogs were still there. Some up on the porch and the others lolling about in the yard.

Seven times seven. She went through the entire multiplication tables, never missing, never hesitating, and she realized what she was doing was a wonder. Since that long-ago day, she had not once multiplied a single number, even in her head.

You do what you do, she thought, you just *do*, and then she dismissed the multiplication tables entirely and concentrated on the situation at hand.

Arnold would come back. Maybe in the next twenty-four hours. It was all that she had. Except... maybe Billy would come? If Arnold had gotten killed or hurt in town in one of his fights, then the sheriff would come to notify her.

She had to get something into the children's stomachs. She thought of Crystal in the pie safe and James beneath the quilt in the bedroom, and the terrible inspiration that had come to her began to shape itself into something tangible. That made her get down on her knees, bow her head low, but the proper words refused to take form. Her thoughts were as dry and empty as the landscape outside the cabin.

Then, in a flash, the thought she had been fighting became whole. The fully realized notion made her legs begin to shake so that she had to sit in the chair, chest heaving as she gulped lungfuls of air, fighting dizziness. She sat there for a long while and then got up and went to a shelf above the pie safe and took down some loose paper she kept there and a pencil. She took it back to the table and began writing, all the while taking care not to look at the body of her little boy lying in front of her.

She wrote for over an hour, occasionally sharpening the pencil with a paring knife. At last, she finished. She walked back over to the shelf and took down a packet of envelopes and came back to the table. She folded the pages she'd written on and placed an equal number of pages into each envelope, sealed them and then wrote on the outside of each the names of her children and on another, *For Sheriff Billy Kliber*. She walked over to the shelf and placed them up on it, standing them up so they could be seen.

That done, she just sat there in the chair looking out onto the moonlit yard, until the murmurs from the other room settled and died down, and then, in the near, small hours of the morning, while the children and the black man slept, she walked over to the pantry on legs that cramped with every step to gather what she needed.

A stewing pot, a length of stout twine, and her machete that lay by the stove. She poured the rest of the rank water into the pot and started a fire in the stove. She put out four small bowls on the table. Using her teeth and right hand, she tied the twine as tightly as she could around her left forearm a few inches above her wrist. She picked up the machete. Eight times eight, she whispered, and raised the machete above her head. Sixty-four, she grunted and swung, the blade whistling through the air.

The End Game Begins…

Billy had slowed to a fast walk. He hadn't been able to sustain the run he'd begun with. He came upon a bend in the road and around it and in front of him was his police car.

The hood was up and the keys were in the ignition. Sacks of groceries were on the back seat. A quick turn of the key told him the problem.

Fuckin' piece of junk, he muttered and began to run again.

As he ran, he kept an eye out for Arnold. He didn't plan on being ambushed like his deputies had been.

Eight miles to go…

It's Getting Bad

Inside the cabin, things were happening. Fast.

Miz Critchin!

Lucious Tremaine's huge frame filled the doorway between the bedroom and the kitchen. He steadied himself as best he could by holding onto the burlap bag that hung down. What he was seeing was Amelia, seated at the table, her machete in one hand and her other hand … separated from her arm and lying on the table next to a stewpot.

Blood was everywhere. Despite the twine she'd bound her arm with, bright red liquid was spurting from it. Amelia was almost completely out, swaying in the chair, fighting to remain conscious and losing the battle.

Lucious moved toward her with deceptive speed, belying both his enormous size and his own near-death condition. He reached her in two steps, just as she slumped forward, finally losing consciousness.

Oh, my Lord! he whispered. Behind him appeared Mandy, taking in the scene, her hand flying to her mouth, her eyes as large as saucers.

Mama! she cried and ran to the black man and her mother. Lucious was clutching Amelia's bloody stump with both his massive hands, applying pressure to stanch the flow of blood. At least for the moment, it seemed to be working. But Mandy could see the man couldn't hold on forever. He was too weak himself. She grabbed his shirt and began to rip it into pieces.

What th', he said.

Shh, she said. I need a tourniquet.

He nodded. Hurry. I can't hold on much longer.

She kept tearing the material and in seconds had four long pieces, which she began tying around her mother's forearm as tightly as she could.

That done, she stepped back. Let go, she said. See if it's tight enough.

He did and it held.

You can't leave it like that, he said. He reached behind him to the wooden box beside the stove where the kindling was and selected a piece of wood about six inches in diameter. He unwound the strip of cloth nearest the stump and rewound it, tying the ends to the stick. He twisted the stick until sufficient pressure was applied to stanch the bleeding and then untied the other pieces of cloth.

There, he said. If you don't release the pressure every few minutes, she'll get gangrene. It should quit bleeding in a bit.

Mandy nodded. She placed her hand over Lucious and said, Let me take it. You need to lie down. But, first—she reached over to put her free arm around her mother's waist—help me get her to the floor to lay down.

Together, they were able to move Amelia from the chair to the floor. She handed the stick to Lucious and ran into the bedroom, coming back with a quilt, which she put over her mother's prone form.

Taking in long, quick breaths, she looked at Lucious. Is she—?

Dead? No. She's in shock. But we've got to get her to a doctor, or she will be.

Mandy nodded. Reality set in. We can't. The dogs won't let us out.

I remember. But we've got to try. Let me rest a bit and then I'll go out with the machete, see what I can do.

Mandy didn't say anything. She knew what he was suggesting was impossible but she didn't want to say that, clinging to the hope that maybe, just maybe … he could accomplish what they'd failed to do. But she knew he couldn't. She couldn't let him go out there.

You can't go out there, she began, those dogs will kill you. You'll be—

A low chuckle came from deep inside his throat. You think those mutts can stop me? It ain't the first time I faced a bunch of mangy mutts like that. I'll wait till it gets dark and then we'll see. He changed the subject. Why did your momma do this? Trying to kill herself?

Her answer was instantaneous. Oh, no! Not Mama! She was trying to feed us. Give us one more meal so we could hold on until help came. We haven't eaten in a long time.

Oh, child, he said. I don't believe I've ever seen a braver woman than that.

There was silence between them for a few seconds and then Mandy said, in a low voice, Me neither.

Lucious looked at the hand still lying on the table. So … should we do what she wanted?

Mandy shook her head violently. No! Never!

Lucious started to say something, but was interrupted by raucous barking and growling that erupted in the front yard. They both went to the window.

Where a strange scene was taking place.

***

Arnold was walking up to the house from the road.

And his dogs were closing in a circle around him.

Arnold's Back

What the hell, he said. Shut up, Rufus! He bent down to pet his favorite bluetick, and got bit for his efforts.

Goddamn you! he yelled. He kicked at the dog and the male pit bull leaped up and sank his teeth into his calf. At once, he was attacked on all sides. Screaming, he pulled out one of his pistols and shot Rufus and began spraying shots all around him, without hitting any of the other dogs. They backed off for a moment and then began circling in closer again. Out of shells with that gun, he reached into a pocket and drew out another one. And ran for the house, firing into the pack as he ran, wounding at least two of his dogs but not killing any.

He lurched up onto the porch, his bluetick Sandy grinding her teeth into his foot and shaking it like a toy. He turned and fired directly into her head and lunged for the door, flung it open and fell inside the room. Mandy ran over and slammed the door shut, catching the pit bull just below his head and kicking at him until he withdrew and she was able to close the door.

Arnold lay on the floor, whimpering and cursing. He looked up and his mouth fell open and he was lost for words.

What the hell's a nigger doing in my house? He pulled himself up to a sitting position and pointed his pistol at him.

Mandy jumped in between them. Get outta my way! Arnold thundered.

No! This is Lucious. He's okay! Don't shoot!

He looked undecided, but kept his gun trained on Lucious.

What's going on? Where are the kids? Who's this guy? Where's your mother?

Abby and Mary are sleeping, Daddy. So is James. Crystal is … dead. And Mama's … she choked back a sob. Mama's on the floor. There.

Arnold stood up. He saw the hand on the table. Jesus Christ! he said. What's that?

It's Mama's.

Jesus H. Christ! What happened? He stepped around the table, saw Amelia on the floor.

This nigger did this, he said.

No. Lucious saved her. He's our friend.

What in the hell is going on? he yelled. Why is Crystal dead? Where is she?

In the pie safe, Mandy said.

She told him all that had gone on since he'd left.

And the dogs won't let us out, she ended with. Now we can get out of here. You'll get us out of here.

I ain't got time for this shit, he said. The sheriff's after me. I'm leaving. And you—he nodded at Mandy—are coming with me.

What? She was horrified. What about Mama?

What about her? She's gonna die, looks like. You're going with me. You're my daughter. You got to do what I say.

I'm not your daughter, Mandy said, the blood draining from her face.

What? Are you crazy?

No. I'm not. Mama told me. I'm Sheriff Billy Kliber's daughter. You're not my father. And I'm not going anywhere with you. You'd have to kill me first.

Arnold snarled and started to say something, but was interrupted by a series of shots outside. He rushed to the window.

All he could see were his beautiful dogs. Falling, one by one as shots rang out. They didn't seem to know where the bullets were coming from and neither did Arnold. But, he had an idea who was shooting.

That sonofabitch!

From just beyond the yard came a voice, yelling. Hello, the cabin. Arnold, come out with your hands up.

man was killing him.

Amelia was lying next to the two men and she came to and forced herself up. Billy gasped at the sight of her. She was covered in blood and then he saw her stump weakly spurting blood, the tourniquet that had been tied having come loose. Mandy came from somewhere behind him and ran to her mother and grabbed her arm in both hands, squeezing until the flow slowed and then stopped. She grabbed the strip of cloth and retied it to her mother's arm.

Billy brought his gun up to bear on the black man's back. Let go of him! he shouted. Amelia made a sound and he saw her trying to say something, unable to get the words out, but shaking her head and giving Billy a look that he read clearly. She wanted Arnold dead.

He had a decision to make. And no time to make it in.

Sheriff! You in there?

It was the deputies.

And Arnold reached up with one last attempt and was able to hook his fingers into Lucious's eye. The black man screamed. He tried to hold on but Arnold, with renewed strength, bucked and slipped out from underneath him. Before Billy could react, Arnold rolled over and in a trice was holding the gun he'd dropped. And, pointed at Billy.

I'll shoot, Arnold said. Then, he did a surprising thing. He whipped his gun around to train it on Amelia. Her, he said. I'll shoot this bitch. Even if you shoot me, I'll get the shot off, Kliber.

Arnold, he said. Give it up, man. My men are here. You'll never make it out of here alive.

Arnold grinned. You're not as smart as you think you are, Kliber. I'm going to walk right out of here. He looked at Mandy. Come over here, darlin'. Come to your daddy.

You aren't my father! she screamed. *He* is. She nodded toward Billy.

Maybe, Arnold said. But he can't help you now. Come over here or I'll shoot Amelia. They'll shoot me, but she'll still be dead.

Don't do it, Mandy, Billy said.

Mandy looked back and forth between the two men and then made up her mind. Lucious, she said. Get Mama's arm. He scuttled to Amelia and took Amelia's arm from her daughter, applying pressure to it. She stood up and limped over to Arnold's side. He reached for her, his arm around her neck and brought the gun to bear on her head.

That's my good girl, he said, smirking. He stepped toward the door and Mandy came with him without any struggle or protest.

We're leaving now, he said to Billy. Tell your men to stand down. Give me ten minutes. I'll turn Mandy loose when I know I'm clear.

No he won't, Amelia whispered hoarsely from where she lay on the floor. He's lying.

Arnold was on the porch now. Holding Mandy with his arm around her neck, he looked out over the yard and saw six deputies in a semicircle, all with their guns drawn. And two civilians, Bear and Teddy.

Billy stepped out behind him.

Let him go, boys, he said. We'll get him.

Arnold nodded, happy. That's right, boys. Let me go. You heard your boss. He forced Mandy to step off the porch, still holding onto her. The pair began to walk backwards, toward the woods behind the cabin. A few feet inside the trees, they disappeared. Two of the deputies started toward the spot they'd been a moment before, but Billy called them back.

We've got some wounded people in here, he shouted. You need to get them to the hospital right now. He stepped off the porch. All except you, Bear. I want you to go with me. You know these woods better'n anyone.

He walked over to one of the two police cruisers and opened the trunk. He took out two rifles and handed one to Bear. He reached back in and grabbed a box of shells and a pair of canteens, handing them to Bear as well.

You got a lighter or matches? he said to the man.

Sure do, Sheriff. Both.

Good. Grab that tarp in the back seat and meet me up at the house. There should be a first aid kit in the glove box. Grab that, too.

Inside the cabin, deputies were placing Amelia on one stretcher and Lucious on another. Someone had reapplied a tourniquet to Amelia's arm. Her face was white and she was unconscious. One of the deputies had the two children by the hand and was leading them to the door.

Good, Billy said. Get them all to town quick as you can. Then, you—he pointed to Teddy—and you—he pointed to George—get supplies and come back here and come find us. We'll try to mark our trail best we can. He added, Get an APB out as soon as you get back. Get the Rangers, have one of these guys fill 'em in. The rest of you men, take care of these bodies in here. Get 'em back to town.

Yessir, Teddy said. Sheriff?

What?

Here's something we found. It's for you. He handed Billy the letter Amelia had placed on the shelf.

Billy took it, stuck it in his pocket and turned to Bear. You ready?

The two men took off at a fast walk and soon disappeared into the woods at the same spot Arnold and Mandy had.

The Big Thicket

The pair alternated running with fast walking, Arnold deciding which pace to use. Ten minutes into their escape, Mandy stopped. You said you'd let me go now. I can't go any more.

Arnold looked at her for a long second and then reached over and slapped her in the face, hard. You better learn somethin' quick, girl. You better just mind me and you better just know you're going with me. You're my new wife.

But … but … I'm your daughter. Legally, she hastily added.

Arnold laughed, a wicked snarl on his face. You're not my daughter, he said. You already tole me that.

I know, but by law I am.

He slapped her again, harder this time. The blow left a distinct red handprint on her cheek. Where we're goin' there ain't no law. 'Cept mine. I'm the law where we're goin'. And my law says we're man and wife.

I can't go on. She sank to the ground.

What's the matter with you?

I haven't eaten or drank anything … in days. I'm hurt.

He reached down and grabbed her arm, yanking her up. Let's go. I'll get you water. Just ahead.

She tried to comply, but her legs refused to work.

Goddamn it! he said. He grabbed her and hoisted her body over his shoulders. You're coming with me.

In five minutes, they emerged from the trees into a swamp. Arnold set her down under a cypress tree and walked to the edge of the water. He took off his shirt and dunked it into the water and then brought it back and handed to her. Just suck on it, he said.

Mandy wanted to refuse but her thirst wouldn't let her. Greedily, she took the sodden shirt and put it to her lips. Arnold gave her a minute and then yanked his shirt back away from her.

That's enough, he said. You'll get sick if you drink too much. Try to walk. I'll get us something to eat but you got to keep moving. I ain't carryin' you. If you can't walk, I can't use you. I'll kill you. That plain enough for you?

She stood on trembling legs. She took one step, then another, her calves cramping, but she fought back the urge to scream at the pain and took another and then another. She forced all thoughts from her mind and simply focused on walking.

Arnold nodded. It was going to work out. He'd get her something to eat and she'd be right as rain. She was going to make a good wife. He just needed to break her spirit a little more.

Where… She fought for the words. Where we going?

None a'yore business. A second later, To a place I know. Cut 'N Shoot. I got a friend there. My old cellmate. He'll help us out.

How far?

Not far. Mebbe ten miles or so.

Then … Siddown! he whispered, and took out the remaining pistol he had in his pocket. Be quiet.

She sank to the ground and watched Arnold creep forward down to the edge of the water. He raised his arm, steadied it and then fired a shot. And then another.

Got it! he shouted, and then seemed to realize he'd made too much noise, disregarding the sound of the two shots he'd just fired. He waded into the water, reached down to grab something and then began to drag it up onto the bank.

It was a gator. A small one, about three feet long.

Now we got somethin' to eat, he said.

He pulled up the carcass to next to her. Don't go away, he said, laughing as she tried to scoot away from it. I'm gonna get some dry wood and build a fire.

***

Both Billy and Bear stopped dead in their tracks and looked at each other.

How far? Bear said.

'Bout a mile, I'd say. Mile and a half, maybe?

Think he—

Don't say it. He mighta just shot a snake or something.

Yeah, Bear said, but both men pushed on at a faster pace, almost running.

***

Just behind the two men, another man labored along at a slower pace. He was unable to maintain a pace nearly as fast as the men in front of him, mostly because his gut burned with the bullet in it. And he also had to follow signs to make sure he was heading in the right direction.

He was moving slower, but with just as much determination.

In the Hospital

In the small hospital in the town of Sugar Hill, Amelia Critchin lay in a bed, tubes protruding from various parts of her anatomy, her left arm swaddled in bandages. She had come to a couple of times, but not for long, lapsing back into unconsciousness each time. In the room next to hers lay two of her remaining children, both of them having had their feeding tubes removed and sitting up in bed and looking cheerful. The nurses on duty kept coming in, smiling and chatting with them. Their room was filled with stuffed animals and toys, contributed by the townspeople who had learned of their plight.

Amelia came to for the third time and this time managed to stay awake.

What happened? she said to the nurse on duty, who was sitting in a chair next to her bed.

The nurse jumped up and pushed a button to alert the doctor. Oh dear, she said. You're awake! Praise God!

Where am I and where are my children? she said. Where's Mandy? Abby and Mary? Where's James? Where's Lucious?

The doctor walked in and his face burst into a smile. Mrs. Critchin! he said. It's good to see you with us. He walked over and picked up her good hand, feeling for her pulse. To the nurse, he said, Go get that deputy at the front desk.

He picked up her chart and began making notations on it, ignoring what

Amelia was asking for at the moment. Finally, he said, Mrs. Critchin, I understand your concerns. Deputy Barclay will be here in a minute and get you up to date on everything. Tell you what—two of your kids are next door and I think they're in good enough condition to bring in. Your son is upstairs in another ward. He's sedated and can't be moved. Nurse? Please go get them and bring the girls here to see their mother.

Lenny walked in and went right over to Amelia. I'm Lenny Barclay, Mrs. Critchin. I'll answer all of your questions.

She looked at him with a puzzled look on her face. You're a deputy? How come—

How come I'm not in uniform? How come I'm in a hospital gown? He laughed. Cause I'm another one of Arnold's victims. Shot me here. He pointed to his stomach. Figured as long as I had to be in here I could be of some use.

There was a brief flurry of noise and a blur of movement as Abby and Mary came flying into the room and over to their mother where both of them jumped up with her. Kids! said the nurse, then the doctor smiled and said, They're okay, Miss Gladstone.

Lenny gave them a few minutes to cry and hug each other and then sat down on the chair the nurse had vacated, and began telling Amelia all that had happened.

By far, the hardest thing was having to tell her about Mandy, and he tried to give her as much reassurance as he could.

Sheriff Billy will find them, he said. You can count on it.

Count on It

Sheriff Billy had, indeed, found them. More accurately, he found Mandy. Arnold was nowhere to be seen.

Mandy! he shouted as he and Bear burst into the clearing. You all right? Where's Arnold?

She rose up on her side, relief shining from her eyes. Sheriff! Thank God!

The two men rushed to her side. Where's Arnold? Billy said.

He's … she looked all around. He was just here. He was going to get some firewood. That way. She sank back down, exhausted.

Oh shit, Billy said. He lifted his rifle and turned in a circle, looking everywhere. He gave a hand signal to Bear who nodded and walked cautiously in the direction Mandy had pointed in, holding his own rifle at the ready.

***

Arnold was only a few steps from emerging into the clearing where he'd left Mandy when Billy shouted. He stopped in his tracks then laid down the armful of wood he'd been carrying and carefully stepped away from the sound of the voices. One of his hunting skills was moving silently and invisibly through the woods. He moved quickly and in seconds was fifty yards away, then he was far enough away he could move faster. When he was what he considered a safe distance, he stopped and positioned himself behind a tree. He wasn't too worried they'd come after him. If the situation had been reversed, he would have given chase, but he knew Billy thought differently. He'd just want to get Mandy to a doctor.

Bitterly disappointed he had lost his new "wife," he knew his pistol was no match against two men who were most likely armed with rifles. He might kill one of them, but not both of them. He decided it made more sense to keep at a distance and then see if he could sneak up on them. That fucking Kliber! The next time they met, things would be different. He vowed they would.

***

Bear came back, shrugging his shoulders. He's long gone, Billy. Musta heard us.

Billy was down on his knees, alongside Mandy. Bear, we've got to get her to the hospital. I don't know how she's gone on this long. She's all bones. That leg looks bad, too.

Let me, Bear said. He leaned over, picked the girl up like she was a sack of potatoes and hoisted her over his shoulder. They pushed on back the way they'd come.

Half a mile later, Bear leaned over and placed Mandy on the ground with her back to a large oak. Gotta take a rest, Billy. Give me a few minutes. Mandy gave a low moan, but didn't wake up. Bear plopped down on the ground, wiping his forehead, which was beaded with sweat.

By way of answer, Billy stepped over and picked her up the same as Bear had done, only not with quite as much ease. Bear nodded and the trio set off again, pushing off through the dense woods.

Billy was able to go nearly a mile before he had to stop to rest.

How far to the cabin you figure? he asked Bear.

Bear started to reply when a figure stepped out from behind a tree ten

just noise.

He nodded and left the room.

The instant the doctor left, Lenny returned.

I heard, Mrs. Critchin. You sure that's what you want?

You, too, Lenny? You want to know why I want a hook and not some "ladylike" cap on it?

Well, it's none'a my bidness…

I'll tell you anyway. As long as that bastard Arnold's out there, I mean to always have me a weapon.

Lenny nodded. You put it that way, I guess I see your point. Maybe I oughta get one, too.

Involuntarily, he put his hand on his stomach stitches. You know, that sonofabitch has kinda soured me on sheriffin'. I been thinkin'—I got me a cousin lives up in Canada, is some kind of reporter. He tells me he can get me a job on the loading dock at his newspaper. I'm thinkin' of goin'.

Amelia looked at him and her eyes softened. Arnold's messed up a lot of people's lives, Lenny. But I'd think hard about that. Good lawmen are hard to come by.

He smiled. Thanks, Miz Critchin. Appreciate that.

She asked him for an odd favor.

Could you get me an ice pick?

An ice pick? What for?

So I'll have something until I can get that hook.

He left and half an hour later returned with her request. They had an extra one in the kitchen he said, handing it over.

She smiled her thanks and then slid it into the sleeve covering her stump and began practicing getting it out quickly. Lenny watched her for awhile, reminded of his own fast draw practices with his pistol.

Showdown

Arnold's finger tightened on the trigger, but before he could pull it, Bear leaped in front of Mandy and at the same time, a huge black shape came out of nowhere and obliterated Arnold's body in the best cross-body block ever seen in the Big Thicket. An NFL-quality tackle.

None of them had seen him come up. Arnold pulled the trigger, but the bullet went harmlessly skyward. He tried to pull the gun up and fire again, but Lucious hit him with a forearm shiver and that was the end of that. He didn't make a sound, just collapsed. It looked like the side of his head was stove in.

Billy was already up and pointing his rifle at Arnold and nearly pulled the trigger before Lucious delivered his blow. It all happened in the space of a second or two. For a few ticks of the clock, Billy considered still pulling the trigger on the unconscious man. Every fiber in his being wanted to, but in the end, he just shook his head and lowered his weapon. He walked over and cuffed him.

Lucious was also down. Although Arnold's shot had gone wide, he didn't look like he could get up. You all right, sir? Billy said. He'd been told the man's name back at Amelia's cabin but he couldn't remember it. It had seemed unimportant at the time. He remembered Amelia saying something about the man saving them.

And, being gutshot.

Billy figured his deputies would get him to town with the others and didn't understand why he was out here.

When asked, Lucious said, The lady saved my life. Figured you folks might need a hand. I seen guys like him before.

Bear chuckled. Looks like maybe you figured right. We owe ya.

Billy said, Can you walk, sir?

The name's Lucious, he said. He managed to get himself up into a standing position. He took a step forward and his legs crumbled beneath him and Billy caught him before he fell.

Maybe I could use a hand, Lucious said. He chuckled, ruefully.

You think you could walk if you leaned on me? Billy asked him.

I think so. But, how you gonna get him back? He nodded at Arnold still lying silent.

Billy thought about the situation. He or Bear was going to have to carry Mandy and one of them was going to have to help Lucious as well. That didn't leave anyone to help with Arnold. He made a quick decision.

We got to get going, he said to Bear. Give me that set of handcuffs I gave you.

Bear handed them over.

Help me get Arnold over to that tree, he said. Together, the two men lifted Arnold's body and brought him over to a good-sized pine tree. They propped Arnold up in his knees—still unconscious—and, uncuffing his hands, wrapped his arms around the trunk of the tree as far as they could go and then hooked both pairs of handcuffs together and attached them to his hands.

There, Billy said. He can't get out of that. We'll send somebody back to pick him up. We've got to get Mandy and Lucious to the hospital.

Billy, you know there are bears out here. Cougars, too, I think. Is it safe to leave him here like this?

Billy just looked at Bear and shook his head.

The four of them set off, Billy carrying the still unconscious Mandy, and Lucious leaning heavily on Bear. Billy figured they were about four miles from the cabin. He stopped for a minute then fired off three quick shots into the air.

We'll go about a mile or so and then do it again, he said. It's the international signal of distress. Just hope someone hears it and comes. He tried to get some water from his canteen into Mandy, who still hadn't come to. She sputtered and choked and he gave it up, hoping she'd gotten down a swallow or two. She didn't look good. He handed it to Lucious, who drank a good five-six swallows before nodding his head in thanks and handing it back. She needs a doctor, he said, and Billy just grunted.

You men go on without me, Lucious said. You can make better time if it's just you two and her.

Billy thought about arguing with him, but he could see he was right. They'd make much better time without him. Looking at Mandy's wan face, it was clear time was precious.

Okay, Lucious. You're right. As soon as we get to the cabin, I'll send some men back to get you. And, Arnold. He shook the man's hand and handed him his canteen.

Lucious took another quick drink and then handed it back. You need it for her. I'll be okay.

Okay, then. Here. For the bears. He handed Lucious the gun he'd taken from Arnold and then he and Bear set off, Mandy limp in Bear's massive arms.

Before they'd gone another mile, they could hear faint shouts from up ahead in the direction they were walking. Billy fired off three more shots and they sat down and waited. Like an echo, three shots sounded faintly within a few seconds.

In fifteen minutes, they were surrounded by deputies and auxiliary deputies. Who'd had the foresight to bring a stretcher. Bear quickly transferred Mandy to it and two men lifted it and looked at Billy expectedly.

Get her to the hospital, Billy ordered. Fast. He leaned over and kissed Mandy on the brow. "Go with God, sweetheart."

It was out of his hands now. He didn't want to think about her chances.

She looked terrible, her face white and her breath faint. She hadn't come to during their entire travel. He had no doubt she was close to death.

He told Bear to go back with the rest of them. He pointed at Ezra, Paul, and Liam Joe Sweeny. You men. You come with me. We have some men to pick up. Somebody give me a gun.

The four men headed back the way he'd just come.

A Big Wind

And suddenly, just like that, the barometric pressure dropped noticeably and the air chilled at least twenty degrees. Clouds, for the first time in weeks, appeared and cast the woods in deep shadow nearly as dark as night. A breeze, then a stout wind came up.

It's a norther, Paul Brazill said.

It's more than a norther, Billy said. It's the granddaddy of all northers. This looks bad.

Indeed it did. The men picked up their pace.

Just as they reached where he'd left Lucious, the tops of the trees began bending then the wind came straight in through the trees as a rain swept down and the wind raised to where the drops weren't falling; they were hurtling sideways. It was all the men could do to stand upright.

Lucious! Billy shouted his name at the top of his lungs, but the sound was swept away the instant it left his lips. From behind a big oak appeared what first looked like a bear but it turned out to be Lucious. Billy and the other three men ran as hard as they could toward the man. An instant before they reached him, a roar sounded that resembled the sound of a freight train.

Get down! yelled Lucious. It's a tornado!

All four men dropped down behind the tree that provided the only shelter to be had.

The gates of hell opened.

Even in the dense woods the wind somehow got through, hurling huge branches and clouds of leaves, dirt and debris at them, even a medium-sized oak tree and a number of smaller pines. They curled up in fetal positions, their heads between their knees. For what seemed an eternity—and was, considering the circumstances—the wind roared over them.

And, just like that, it was over. The roar began to diminish as the tornado moved away.

Anybody hurt? Billy said, brushing debris and standing up.

We're okay, Billy, Paul said.

Except they weren't. Billy and two of his deputies along with Lucious stood, but one man remained on the ground.

Liam Joe Sweeny didn't move. Liam worked as a butcher in Langdon's General Store and was a volunteer deputy in the auxiliary as well as serving as a volunteer fireman. A smallish man, maybe 5'6" and weighing about 125 pounds, he lay where he'd dropped to the ground.

Liam? Billy stood over the prone figure. He turned to the others. I don't think he's hurt, he said. Maybe he just fainted. He prodded the man with his foot. C'mon, Liam. It's all right. It's passed over.

But Liam didn't move. Billy reached over to pull the man up to a sitting position and then dropped him like a burnt match that had just reached his fingers. My God! he said.

Someone else picked up the man and turned him over. One of the other deputies began retching. Liam looked fine, looked like he was just sleeping … and then they all saw it. A sliver of wood, no more than half an inch in diameter, about the size of a pencil, was sticking out from between his eyes. There wasn't any blood, but it looked as if he was dead.

Jesus, said two of the men in unison. Little Liam Joe, another man whispered as if he was standing in church.

And suddenly, Liam Joe sat up, looked around blinking his eyes and said, Is it lunchtime yet?

They all laughed in relief and Liam seemed to realize something was sticking in his face—his eyes crossed as he tried to make out what it as—and he reached up and plucked out the splinter. It had gone in less than half an inch and when he removed it, a single drop of blood rolled out.

Something occurred to Billy. He wondered if the others had been able to get Mandy out and on her way to the hospital before the tornado struck. For a bit, he considered turning around and going back to the cabin to see if she was gone and okay, but in the end he knew where his duty lay.

Come on, he said to the men. Let's go. We've got to get Critchin.

He told one of the men to stay with Lucious and they'd return to pick them up on their way back.

Maybe the tornado picked him up and dropped him in Hell, muttered Paul. The others nodded in grim agreement as they set off, picking their way over downed trees and other debris.

The Dream

After Lenny left her to resume his post outside her door, Amelia lay in the hospital bed playing with the ice pick. After a bit, drowsiness overtook her and she fell asleep.

And dreamed.

The old dream—the one with the big black man—Lucious?—and the machete and the darkness and fire and brimstone. This time, it was she who held the machete and Lucious was up and to her right, in an elevated position. It looked like he was behind a pulpit and appeared to be preaching. She could see his lips move and spittle flying and beads of sweat on his brow, but she couldn't hear what he was yelling. All about them lightning flashed and there were burning fires scattered throughout the darkness. Hell.

She woke in a start, her heart pumping fast, but it wasn't fear she felt. Something else she couldn't put her finger on. Anticipation? Something good about to happen? Something bad? She didn't know, but she knew it would be momentous. She wished her mother was still alive so she could ask her what it meant. After a bit, she fell asleep again and this time slept a dreamless slumber.

Tornado Passes

Twenty minutes after the tornado had passed, Billy and his men reached where he'd handcuffed Arnold to the pine tree.

The tree was gone.

As was Arnold.

You sure this is where he was? said Ezra.

He wasn't entirely sure until he took another, more careful look around.

Yes, he said. I remember that big oak there. He walked over to where he thought the pine tree had been. Yes. This is it. Six inches above the ground level, there was the stump of the pine. It was sheared off almost as cleanly as if a saw had cut it down.

Christ! Paul took off his hat and wiped his brow with a handkerchief. That's some fucking wind!

Billy told the two men to cast about and see if they could find out where the tree—and Arnold—had been blown to. In widening circles, all three men walked in ever widening orbits from the stump. A hundred yards out and no sign of either.

And, then…

Over here, Sheriff!

Billy and Ezra ran to where Paul was standing.

He'd found the tree.

But, no Arnold.

They widened the search another hundred yards from the tree, but still no Arnold. Paul bent down and lifted the tree.

There, he said. The other two men looked. What was clearly a bootprint was just underneath it.

He got away, Billy said.

Looks like, Paul said.

Billy thought for a moment. Should they go after him? They didn't have a clue what direction to go in. Shaking his head, he said, No. It's no use. Let's get back. We'll come back when we have more men and some supplies. I bet he's on his way to Cut 'N Shoot. It's the only place he can find someone to cut those cuffs off. We'll find him.

He said that to his men, but privately he had doubts. He didn't think Arnold would quit until he had exacted his vengeance on Amelia and taken Mandy away with him. That was the real reason he ordered them back. Out here, he was on Arnold's turf and at a disadvantage. Back in town he had a better chance. The more he thought about it, the more he was convinced that if Arnold had survived the tornado—and it appeared that he had—he was more and more sure, in his bones, that he wasn't on his way to Cut 'N Shoot, but back to Sugar Hill and the hospital.

As they left the clearing on their way back to the cabin, he took one last look around. For a fleeting second, he thought he saw a tiny movement behind a huge oak to the left of the clearing, and considered checking it out, but decided it was probably just a figment of his imagination, so he turned around and they walked back to the cabin. He couldn't stop worrying about Mandy. A sense of urgency overcame him and he urged his men to move faster.

Amelia and Billy

When Amelia awoke, it was dark. The night sounds of a hospital brought her back to where she was. Muffled voices out in the hall, a beeper going off somewhere, the squeak of a gurney going by with a bad wheel. As her eyes grew accustomed to the darkness, she saw a man. Sitting in a chair in the corner, slumped over. Asleep. It almost looked like—

Amelia? You awake?

Billy.

Oh, Billy! She struggled to sit up, but before she could Billy had risen and rushed to her side. He sat on the edge of her bed and took her hand in his. Amelia! You're going to be fine, the doctor said.

She smiled and, hard as she tried, she couldn't stop the tears that came to her eyes. I guess, she said. Except for… She raised her arm with the missing hand and Billy dropped everything and reached for it. He drew it to him and kissed the bandaged stump.

This? He laughed. This just makes you even more interesting, he said. His smile faded. I have to talk to you about something. Arnold's still out there. And—

You think he's headed for here. For the hospital, she finished for him.

Well, yeah. I think—

That he wants to take Mandy. And … kill me.

Billy nodded.

Amelia nodded back. That's why I had Lenny give me this. She pulled out the ice pick and then put it back in her sleeve. I had a dream.

A dream?

Yes. You don't need to know about it. It's a dream I've been having for a long time. Years. I think it's about to come to an end.

They were quiet for a moment.

Are my kids okay?

Billy nodded. The girls are staying with Missus Beauler in town. She's really nice and loves kids. They're just fine. And James and Mandy are here in the hospital and should be able to leave soon.

Is Lucious okay?

He nodded. Yes, he is. He had the bullet removed and they say he'll be fine. He's a strong man. He's just down the hall, in fact. You want to see him?

He's here? She was incredulous. But, this is a white hospital.

Billy grinned. And your friend Lucious just broke the color barrier. He had a little help.

You?

Yeah. Kind of. They wanted to send him to the Negro clinic over in Niggertown. I had a little talk with the doctors and they agreed to admit him here. Not that they aren't okay over there, but they don't have the equipment they do here.

I'd like to have heard that conversation.

He smiled. Well, yeah. It got a little bit loud, but it's the right thing to do. Main thing is, I think if Arnold does come back, Lucious is somebody he'd like to take care of too. And, I don't have a man to spare to watch him over there.

Thank you, Billy. And, yes, I'd like to see him if he's awake.

If he isn't, we'll just wake him.

She swung her legs over the side of the bed and stood up.

Billy? she said.

Yes?

You remember that day you came to our place and Arnold stuck your horse with his gig?

I sure do.

You remember you asked if I wanted to leave with you?

Yes.

I wish … I wish I had.

She leaned on him and he put his arm around her and they walked down the hall to Lucious's room.

Halfway there, Billy reached down and brushed a strand of hair out of her eyes. I wish you had, too, Amelia. I've wished that every day since.

Then he said something that made her come close to tears.

Thank God it's not too late.

She stopped and inclined her head to look up at him but didn't say anything.

Arnold Escapes

When the tornado hit, Arnold didn't try to break loose from the tree. He'd already tried that and knew it was useless. He stood, facing the onrushing wind and the trees, branches and other debris it brought with it, defiant, almost as if it were a man rushing to fight him.

Fuck you, God! he shouted, as it reached him. You can't kill me!

A sapling, coming at him like it was a spear launched by Thor, struck him between the eyes and he went down.

That was all he remembered until he awoke ten minutes later. Lying on his stomach, his face down in the dirt.

And, his arms free. The tree he'd been cuffed around was gone. The handcuffs were still on him, but other than that, he was free.

He lurched to his feet, unsteadily. Yeah! he growled. Can't beat me, can you!

He began walking toward the direction of Cut 'N Shoot.

An hour later, he came upon a cabin in the woods. There didn't appear to be anyone there. Cautiously, he approached it. When he got near, he picked up a length of wood lying in the yard. With that as a weapon, he crept up on the cabin. He pushed open the door, hard, and stepped in, the piece of wood at the ready.

It was deserted.

In a toolbox over in a corner, he found a hacksaw. In less than two minutes, he'd cut off the handcuffs. Rummaging through the cabin, he found a pie safe and in it a hunk of deer jerky wrapped in waxed paper. Ravenous, he tore at the meat and had it down in seconds, half-chewed. Satiated, he resumed his search and was rewarded by finding a Bowie knife in a sheath, hidden underneath the thin mattress on the only bed. He figured the cabin was most likely a hunting cabin and not one where someone lived.

He sat down at the lone chair in front of a roughly hewn table and thought about his options.

He could go on to Cut 'N Shoot. There was a guy lived there he'd celled with years ago in Huntsville he was sure would help him out.

Or, he could finish what he started out to do and get Mandy and take her with him. And, kill her mother, that bitch, Amelia. Be nice to take care of that bastard Billy, too. He was pretty sure they'd be at the hospital in Sugar Hill.

He thought about each option and made his decision.

Two hours of hiking through the woods brought Arnold to the first outlying houses in Cut 'N Shoot.

But he hadn't come there to find his old friend.

He'd come there to find a car. It was the closest place where he could get one.

There was a green Studebaker sitting beside the very first house he came to, a white frame building in some disrepair. The house next to it was half a block away. Perfect.

He watched from the safety of the trees for awhile. After an hour, the front door opened and out came an old man, moving slowly and with a limp. Headed toward the Studebaker.

Arnold ran toward him, the Bowie held behind his back. He covered the twenty-five yards in seconds, and came up to the man, smiling.

Hey, he said.

Startled, the man jumped and looked up, instantly wary. Hey, yourself, he said. Whatcha want?

Your car, Arnold said. He brought out the knife. And your money.

The man backed up. Hey ... fuck you.

Yeah? You lookin' to die, old-timer?

He didn't say anything, just kept his eye on Arnold's knife.

Anybody in the house?

No.

Let's just go see to be sure. Gimme your keys first.

He followed the man inside. He was telling the truth.

Just take the car and go, the man said.

I am, Arnold said. Count on it. Give me your money.

The man stared at him. I don't have much money. I had to retire. Bum leg.

Arnold laughed. Yeah, well, I don't much care about that. Give me what you got.

The man pulled out his billfold and handed it over.

Arnold looked through it, pulled out some bills. This it? Twelve stinkin' bucks?

Yeah. I was on my way to buy groceries. What am I gonna eat now?

Arnold's answer was to step toward him and twist his arm around his back. Down, he ordered and the man sank to his knees before his couch. Arnold grabbed a lamp on an end table and tore the cord off and used it to bind his hands behind him. That done, he went into the kitchen, keeping an eye on the man as he rummaged through drawers in the cabinet. He found an extension cord and brought it back and bound the man's feet together. He picked him up and threw him face down onto the couch. He took the knife and smacked the man hard on the back of his head with the hilt. He had to hit him twice before he went out. He thought about killing him but decided he'd be long gone before the old guy could get loose and get help.

Quickly, he searched the rest of the house. In the one bedroom, he got lucky and found a loaded .38 revolver in a nightstand beside the bed. There was a box of shells and he grabbed those, too.

On his way out, he went by the couch where the old guy was starting to stir. He cracked him again on the back of the head with the man's own gun this time and left.

In a little over two hours, he was pulling into a parking place a block away from the hospital. He didn't want to risk being seen by a deputy. He figured they were on the premises somewhere. He'd made a stop at a general store and made some purchases with the old man's money.

Time to get to work.

Time to get him a new wife, get rid of the old one.

Settle some scores.

His eyes glittered at the thought.

Billy Marshalls Forces

At the hospital, a nurse wheeled Mandy into Lucious's room where her mother and Billy both were.

Mama!

Oh, Mandy! The two women hugged.

In his bed, Lucious grinned. Now, that's a sight for these old eyes. It's good to see a daughter with her mother. He lost his smile for a minute as if thinking of something, but brightened up quickly.

Billy asked the nurse if they had any chairs and she disappeared and came back a few minutes later with a pair of folding chairs for him and Amelia.

When they sat down, Billy told them what was going on.

There's no way of telling, but I have a feeling we haven't seen the last of Arnold, he said. So, there's two deputies who are going to be watching out for him. One at the front desk and another one to keep an eye on all three of you and kind of roam the halls. I'll be in and out myself, so you'll be well protected. I'm going to ask the doctors if they'll put you all in one room. That'll make it easier. And, this may all be for nothing. If he's smart, he's lit out for safer parts.

He left to find a doctor to make the arrangements.

And quickly ran into an obstacle.

Sheriff, I can put Amelia and her daughter in the same room, but not the

Negro. He shouldn't even be in the hospital, but if I put him in a room with two white women, they'll burn this hospital down.

Billy saw there was no budging the man. Can you put Lucious in the room next to theirs? he said.

Well, I'd feel better if I could put him on the second floor with your two deputies and the boy, but, yes, I'll put him next door. Only for a day or two. After that, I'm afraid I'll have a riot on my hands. If not from the town, then from some of the nurses and maybe even a doctor or two. I'm sorry.

Billy nodded and shook hands with the doctor. Thanks, Doc. I know how it is. There wasn't much else he could do.

It's okay, Sheriff. It was Lucious, who'd sat up in his bed while the discussion was going on. I can go back down to the colored hospital, you know.

This is crazy, Amelia said and Mandy nodded her own head vigorously. Hospitals are supposed to take care of the sick. Colored people get just as sick as white folks.

Lucious chuckled. It's fine, Missy. I'm about all healed up anyway. Figure I'll be out in another day or two anyway. Besides, he added. The biggest problem is the food. I don't know how much longer I can eat the food they got here. I got a feeling the colored hospital's chow's a heap more tasty. This is a for-real hardship, y'know.

That broke the tension and they all broke out laughing, even the doctor.

He decided to leave Lucious in the room he was already in and move the two women into the room next to it, which, fortuitously, was already empty. The move was accomplished quickly—simply a matter of a nurse helping them with their few possessions and putting them away in the closet. That done, a single deputy, stationed outside both rooms, could keep watch on both of them at once.

***

Amelia watched all this with trepidation. She knew exactly what Arnold was capable of, how his mind worked. Like Billy, she was sure he'd show up at the hospital. She'd known it all along, which was why she'd wanted the doctor to fit her with a hook. She was positive she'd need a weapon like it. They wouldn't allow her to keep her machete in the hospital. The ice pick helped ease her mind somewhat.

She was also certain that the only way she'd ever feel safe again—both for herself and for Mandy and even Lucious—was only possible by killing Arnold.

A memory drifted into her mind. The night of their wedding. Without a place of their own yet, they had to stay with Arnold's parents until their own cabin was built. They'd been given the use of Arnold's bedroom, right next to his parents' bedroom. The walls were paper-thin and Amelia hadn't wanted to have sex until they had the privacy of their own home.

No, Arnold, she whispered, when he tried to take her nightshift off. They'll hear.

So what? he said. Maybe I want 'em to hear. You're my wife now and you have to do your wifely duty. Everybody knows that. It's in the Bible. So, just shut up.

She jumped up from the bed. I'm going home.

Like hell you are, he snarled. You're my property and you'll do what I say.

He grabbed her by her hair and threw her back down on the bed and grabbed her nightgown around the neck and yanked it until it ripped. She fought as best she could but he was much stronger than her. In the end she endured his thrusting, straining to keep as quiet as she was able, but the whimpers she couldn't control must have been heard in the other room. While Arnold was essentially raping her, his father appeared at the doorway.

What the hell's going on here? he thundered.

Nothing, Daddy, Arnold said, turning his head toward his father. Just doing my husbandly duty.

All right, son, he said. Just keep her damn mewling down. Your mother and I are trying to sleep.

She remembered Arnold turning his face back to her and saying, You heard him. Keep your mouth shut. You might learn to like it if you'd keep your yap shut. You're mine and you better get used to it. This is what husbands and wives do.

And that became the standard by which she conducted her married life. The standard she'd been taught to follow all of her life—by her own parents, by the culture she lived in. Until that day when he'd forced anal sex upon her. That had been the first ... and only .. time she'd ever defied him. That was the day she began to emerge from the darkness.

Never again was she going to do anything for Arnold, no matter what vows she might have to break. It wasn't right the way he'd treated her. And now wanted to do to her daughter. He was like a copperhead snake and there was only one way to deal with something like that.

Kill it.

Billy Has to Leave

Billy came back into her room. He crossed over to sit on her bed. This place is starting to look like a field hospital, he said. You, Mandy, James, Lucious, and I've got two of my men up on the second floor. Not to mention your two girls.

All because of Arnold, she said, a statement, not a question.

Yes. And, there's my deputy he killed.

Her eyes began to brim over with tears. I should have killed him when I had the chance, she said.

I should have let Lucious kill him when he had the chance, Billy said.

In spite of herself, she laughed. I'd say he's used up all his chances.

He smiled at her. Way more.

They were quiet for a bit and then Billy cleared his throat. I've got to tell you something.

She lifted her eyes to his and waited.

I'm going to have to leave here for a little while. But you'll be all right. I'm taking one of my deputies with me but the other one—Lenny—will be here. I'll have him stay right here in the room with you.

Oh, Billy! Do you have to leave? Her face twisted with fear.

He nodded. Yes. I have to. They're burying Eugene. I have to be there.

Her chin quivered. Yes. You do. They're burying Crystal tomorrow. I understand.

They'd completely understood in holding off the burial of Crystal until she and Mandy were strong enough to attend. By tomorrow, the doctor said he thought they could go.

You'll be okay, he said. I shouldn't be gone more than an hour, hour and a half.

She smiled at him. You go, Billy. We'll be okay. Arnold's still out in those woods. He couldn't have walked here this quickly.

That's what Billy figured, too. Still, he had a bad feeling, but what could he do?

He kissed her on the forehead and left the room. Before he left for the funeral, he made one more stop.

Lucious, he said, shaking the man awake. He waited until the man sat up. Lucious, I have to go to a funeral. I'm leaving Deputy Barclay to watch Mandy and Amelia in their room, but I want to do one more thing.

He told the man to hold up his right hand and he swore him in as a deputy. That done, he handed over a police issue .38. Just keep an eye on them until I get back, he said.

I will, Sheriff. You can count on me.

I know I can, Lucious.

And he left.

He stopped at the front desk to instruct Lenny to go to the women's room and stay there until he returned.

On his way out of the hospital, he saw an old man inching his way up the handicapped ramp on crutches. He was dressed in overalls and wore a wide-brimmed hat, the kind fisherman wore for the sun. He had sunglasses on, the kind that almost looked like the glasses blind people wore. He nodded at the man and the man nodded back. There was something a bit off about the man, but he forgot him almost immediately. He paused for a minute to look back and saw him still inching up the slight incline and then decided it was only because he didn't know him. Most likely the guy was from out of town, visiting a relative. Billy shook his head violently to rid himself of cobwebs, clear his mind. He needed to think straight. Get this funeral over with and get back as soon as possible. He climbed in his squad car and pulled away.

Arnold Visits the Hospital

Behind the front desk, the nurse on duty looked up at the elderly man entering the building. I'm sorry, sir, she said. Visiting hours aren't until four o'clock.

It was the last words she uttered before the man leaped over the counter and twisted her neck like a chicken.

I'm just a rebel, Arnold said, as he eased her down to the floor where she couldn't be seen. I can't wait for regular visiting hours. He looked at the board behind her with the room numbers and the names of patients in them.

What the—! Amelia's name wasn't on it. Nor was Mandy's.

And then he understood. They were registered under phony names. Like … they'd been expecting him….

Which meant he had to work quickly. He didn't know where Billy had been headed but he might be back any minute. Which wasn't a bad thing. As long as he was ready for him. And, he meant to be.

He looked at the board with new insight. "Mrs. Smith and Ms Smith" looked like a good bet. Room 118.

Before he went to Room 118, he looked around until he found what he wanted. Luckily, the halls were deserted. Within seconds, he had it. A utility closet in which he grabbed a mop and bucket and, even better, a pair of white hospital overalls, complete with name tag that read Joe Lansdale, and a white cap.

Two minutes later what appeared to be a janitor came out into the hall and started toward Room 118 with a mop and bucket. Two doors from his destination, the door opened and a deputy sheriff came out and closed the door behind him, turned and walked down the hall toward the far end. When he opened the door to another room, the janitor saw it was the men's bathroom. He strode forward and entered Room 118 with a mop and bucket. His head was lowered as he took out the mop and sloshed water onto the floor.

Hello, said Mandy. Amelia started to do the same but something about the man arrested her words and a puzzled look was instantly replaced with one of horror.

It's Arnold! she gasped, and Arnold thrust the mop from him and pulled out a revolver from his pocket. A grin spread wide across his face.

Hey, darlin', he said.

The door opened and Deputy Barclay came in … to a revolver pointed directly at him.

Git your ass down on the floor, Arnold said. Lenny hesitated a second, his hand moving a bit toward his holster.

You don't want to do that, Arnold said. Git down now or you're a dead man. I already kilt you once and you know I'll do it again.

Lenny slid down to a sitting position. Arnold walked over and, keeping his gun trained on the man's head, reached down and took his gun out of its holster. Gimme those cuffs, he said, and Lenny complied. Arnold snapped one end to his wrist and the other to the empty bed near the door, to its frame. That done, he smacked his lips like he'd just eaten a tasty snack, and went over and sat down on his wife's bed.

Nice t'see ya again, darlin'. Miss me?

He turned to stare at Mandy in the bed opposite. Now you, sugar, he said to her. You need to get up and get dressed. You're goin' with me.

Arnold. Amelia spoke his name and he looked at her. Mandy isn't going anywhere with you. She can't walk. And even if she could she's not going anywhere with you.

He grinned. Oh, but you're wrong, he said. That's exactly what she's gonna do. If she doesn't… He left the words unsaid, but it was clear what he meant. To make sure they understood him, he leaned over and placed his gun underneath Amelia's chin. Now, he said. Git your clothes on, Mandy.

She didn't say anything, just threw her sheet off and sat up, swinging her legs over the side of the bed. The flash of naked legs seemed to excite him and he leaned forward as if to get a better look. At the same time, Amelia withdrew her hand from underneath the covers and launched a murderous and swift swipe with the ice pick at his head. It was so quick Arnold never saw it coming until the last split-second. She connected and he screamed. He threw both hands up toward the wound in his face, and inadvertently squeezed the trigger on his gun. It boomed next to his ear and deafened him, and the pain he felt, both from the gunshot to his eardrums and the sharp, sudden pain to his cheek, caused him to drop the gun on the bed. He rolled off the bed to his knees, clutched his face in his hands and moaned.

Amelia stared at the ice pick as if it had betrayed her, then shook her head to clear it and snatched Arnold's gun up and laid it on her lap. She dropped the ice pick beside the gun and reached for the tote sack beside her and felt around in it for something. No one watched her. All eyes were on Arnold. So quickly no one noticed, she brought something out of her sack and fumbled awkwardly with it and the gun. Having the use of only one hand made things difficult, but she managed to put whatever it was she took out of her tote and slide it down into the gun barrel. She laid the gun back down on the bed beside her.

Several things happened simultaneously. The door burst open and in rushed Lucious, gun drawn, assessing the situation, finding Arnold on the floor and running over to where he lay, still moaning, his fingers over the gash in his cheek. Behind him in rushed Billy.

Lucious cocked the gun Billy had given him and laid the barrel on Arnold's head behind his ear.

No! Billy shouted. Don't shoot him, Lucious.

Lucious didn't move. He kept the gun trained on Arnold's head. Mandy came forward a couple of steps, also pointing her gun on Arnold. Amelia slid out of the bed and bent over to Arnold and raised her ice pick to deliver another blow to the man.

Meanwhile, Arnold continued to shrink into himself and whimper.

Stop, Lucious said to Amelia.

All of you stop, Billy said. I'm taking this man into custody. He unhooked the handcuffs on his belt and leaned over to put them on Arnold.

No, Lucious said. This man needs killing. He doesn't deserve prison. He's an animal and he needs to be put down like the rabid dog he is.

He looked at Amelia. Not by you, he said. You've got two daughters by this man. You kill him and they'll always look at you with shame.

Not you, either, Sheriff. I see the way you look at Amelia. How are you going to look in her daughter's eyes if you kill their birth father? How are you going to look at Amelia if you allow him to live, even if it's in prison?

He looked at Mandy. How are you going to feel if you kill him? Even if he wasn't your father, for most of your life you thought he was.

No, he said. The only one who can save this family is me.

If you shoot him I'll have to arrest you, Lucious, Billy said. He stepped toward the two men and stopped when Deputy Barclay spoke up. Sheriff, he said, I saw Critchin shoot at Lucious. I saw it as self-defense.

Two other voices spoke, almost as one.

That's what I saw too, said Mandy. Me, too, said Amelia. If he shoots him, it's definitely self-defense.

Billy smiled. I hear what you folks are saying, he said. But that's not what happened. Lucious, you shoot him, I'm taking you in. I have no choice. I'm the law.

It was a stalemate.

Until Amelia spoke up.

Don't shoot him, Lucious, she said. He's not worth your life.

Before anyone else could speak or do anything, Billy stepped forward and slapped one of the cuffs on Arnold's right hand and the other to the bedpost. As soon as he was secured, Lucious looked at Billy and handed over the revolver. Big mistake, Sheriff, he said. Big mistake.

Barclay, Billy said. Go get a doctor to patch Arnold up. Then, get him over to the jail.

Deputy Barclay, nodded, grim-faced, then left the room. He returned in less than two minutes with a physician. Ten minutes later, Barclay walked away with Arnold securely cuffed to him. Going out the door, Arnold sent a parting shot. You shoulda kilt me, he said, grinning back over his shoulder at Lucious. Y'all're soft, he added. Y'all're all soft.

From nowhere, Amelia appeared behind the pair. In her hand, she held Arnold's revolver.

Uncuff him, she ordered Deputy Barclay. Behind her gathered Billy, Lucious, and Amelia. She trained the revolver on Barclay. He looked at Billy with helpless eyes. Billy hesitated and then nodded.

Go ahead, Deputy, he said. Uncuff him.

Amelia, he said. Don't do this. Don't kill him. He's not worth it. He's—

Before he could finish, Arnold reached forward, snatched the gun from her and spun her around. She fell to the floor.

I tole y'all y'all was soft, he said. Soft and ... stupid.

Amelia looked up at him from where she lay on the floor.

Stupid, Arnold? she said.

Who's got the gun, Amelia?

Give it up, Arnold. Billy, from behind Amelia.

Arnold laughed. I don't think so, Billy. He turned slightly, training the gun on Barclay.

Join your friends, Deputy, he said. He watched while Barclay stepped over to Amelia, as if to shield her from his gun. Arnold laughed. Back there, he said. With your boss. Amelia's goin' with me. He jerked his arm back, indicating she was to come forward.

I'm not going anywhere, Arnold, she said. Not with you. Not ever.

Fuck you, you stupid cow, he said. With that he pointed the revolver at her and pulled the trigger and ... his face disappeared. What was left of the revolver dropped from his hand and his body toppled.

Stunned silence. And then … Billy stepped forward. He motioned to Lenny. Lenny would you get some help and take this trash out of here. He poked at Arnold's body with his foot.

Tamales

The next morning, Amelia sat down with Billy in his office. All of the deputies had been sent out of the room. She'd come at his request.

Amelia, Billy said. I've got to talk to you about something. I wonder if you know what this is? He handed her a twisted piece of metal. She didn't look at it, but nodded her head. Yes, it's mine.

I thought so, he said. It's the pen you won in the sixth grade, isn't it?

What makes you think that?

Well, it says *The pen is mightier than the...* and then it's cut off.

That doesn't mean anything.

You're right. But below that it says *Amelia Lax...* It's cut off but I'm pretty sure if it was all here it'd say your last name....

What're you saying, Billy?

You know what I'm saying, Amelia.

What?

I'm saying that Arnold was a really stupid man.

She smiled.

Maybe, she said.

He smiled back.

Ten minutes later, Amelia gone back to the hospital, Lucious sat down with Billy in his office.

Lucious, Billy said. I've got to talk to you about some things. I've been asked to provide your fingerprints to the Texas Rangers. It's a customary thing for a shooting like this. They've got everyone else's but yours.

He watched for Lucious's reaction. The man was hard to read. It looked as if he blinked a little harder than usual at the news, but that was all.

Okay, he said, trying a different tack. I've got the feeling that you've got a history. Is that possible?

Lucious sat there for a minute, deep in thought, and then seemed to make a decision.

Well, Sheriff … if my prints just stay in Texas, I don't have no worries.

Billy nodded. I see. Usually, that's the protocol, but in this case the ranger led me to think that they may broaden the net a bit. It seems they have some kind of suspicion about you. Sorry, but I think if you were white, that would be it. But…

Lucious nodded. I get you, Sheriff. I get you.

He sighed deeply and then began. It took over an hour to tell him everything and when he was done, his forehead was pouring sweat.

He stood up. I guess my life's in your hands, sir. You want me to go into that cell? I'm pretty much done with running.

Billy sat for a long minute, staring at the floor. Finally, he stood up. Here's what I'm going to do, Lucious. First, I need to take your prints. Can't get out of that.

That done, he put his hand on Lucious's arm and steered him toward the door.

A few minutes later, they were at the hospital. Both Amelia and Mandy were scheduled to be released at noon, an hour from then. He guided Lucious to their room and indicated with his head he was to enter. Half an hour, Lucious, he said. I'll be back. He closed the door quietly behind the man.

Half an hour later, as promised, he showed back up at the door and nodded to Lucious, who gave Amelia a hug and he left with him.

**

Precisely at noon, Billy re-entered Amelia and Mandy's room.

They're ready to check you out, he said. We have to go to the front desk. We'll pick up the girls and then we'll go to the funeral.

While Amelia was signing forms, she turned to Billy and said, They don't have any charges for us? She said it as a question.

That's all been taken care of, he said. And, this is good timing. I lost my tenants at my farm and I figure y'all can just move right in. If that's okay with you, we'll stop by and pick up the girls. James will need to stay here another couple of days and then he'll join us. Do some grocery shopping, too. I don't think there's anything to eat there.

On the way to pick up the girls, he turned to Amelia, who was sitting in the front seat with him. Mandy was in the back seat.

I guess since you're a widow now, you'll have gentlemen callers.

What! Amelia blushed mightily. Whatever would make you think that?

In the back seat, Mandy giggled.

Mandy spoke up. Where's Lucious, Billy? Is he going to live with us there, too?

Billy said, I don't think so, Mandy. If he stayed on the bus I put him on, he's a good ways closer to Mexico than he was a little bit ago. By the time we get y'all settled at the house, I figure he's going to be trying to figure out how to say "tamale" in Mexican.

Tamale, Mandy said.

What?

Tamale, she repeated. That's how you say it in Mexican.

And Spanish, said Amelia.

And Spanish, repeated Mandy.

And English, said Amelia.

They all broke up laughing.

Billy reached over and put his hand on Amelia's arm, just above where her hand should have been, and squeezed. She blushed, fiercely.

Here we are, he said. He pulled the car up a driveway and out ran Mary and Abby, squealing like … well, like excited little girls, followed by a smiling middle-aged woman who was wiping her hands off with her apron.

Mama!

Mama!

Both Amelia and Mandy were out of the car, Amelia's arms around both girls.

What pretty dresses! she said. Abby curtsied and then her sister mimicked her and everyone laughed.

Missus Beauler made 'em for us, Mary said.

The woman blushed. They's good girls, she said. It's a pleasure to have 'em stay with me. The girls ran to her and put their arms around her.

It began to rain—hard—and the girls screamed gaily and they all ran to the car and climbed in.

As Billy pulled away, Mary said, Where we goin', Mama?

Amelia looked back and hesitated. Then, she said, We're going home, darlin.' She paused. Our new home.

Will Daddy be there? Abby said.

She hesitated. No, child. Your daddy's gone.

The child surprised her. Good. I don't like Daddy.

Me either, said Mary. He's mean.

Children, the reason your daddy's not coming home is … he's … dead. He's passed away.

There was silence for a bit.

I'm sorry about that, Mama, Mary said. But I'm not sorry he's not coming home.

Me either.

Abby chirped up. Is there going to be a funeral?

Yes. There's also going to be a funeral for Crystal. Later on this afternoon.

Do we have to go? I mean, to Daddy's?

I think so. He's still your father.

Okay.

Okay.

Is our new house big?

Well, compared to your old one, it's huge, Billy said. You'll each have your own room.

It took a second for that to sink in.

And, then…

Oh boy!

Wow!

And a bed?

Yes, a real bed.

They rode the rest of the way in silence, the girls considering the fact of their own beds, an astounding thing to think about.

When they pulled up in the driveway to the old Faulkner place, Mary and Abby both jumped out of the car and ran, squealing to the house and into it. Mandy stayed behind for a moment, then walked quickly to the door and inside.

They want to pick out their bedrooms, Amelia said.

Billy's eyes twinkled. Think they'll like it here?

She turned to him. They'll love it, Billy. How long?

How long what?

How long can we stay here?

It began to rain, softly at first and then transformed into a hard downpour.

Billy grabbed her hand. Let's go—run!

Amelia stopped, looked up at the sky.

No, she said. I want to feel it. She put her face up to the sky and smiled as the raindrops pelted her. This feels wonderful.

He didn't let go of her hand.

To answer your question…

What?

Your question. How long can you stay here.

Oh.

The answer's up to you, Amelia. I hope it's forever.

Springtime

In January, a postcard from Mexico came to the sheriff's office addressed to Billy. It showed a pristine beach and a fisherman standing beside a giant marlin. It wasn't signed, but Billy knew who it was from. He took it home and showed it to Amelia, who looked at it, smiled and handed it back. This makes me happy, she said. Me too, said Billy, and put it in his pocket.

When March rolled around, Amelia was up on a new tractor Billy had purchased, plowing her field and getting it ready to be tilled to prepare the ground for planting corn.

The rains had been coming every other day, slow, gentle downpours that had filled Boudreaux Creek until it was swollen and ready to burst its banks.

Amelia climbed down off her tractor and walked over to the creek and sat down on its bank. The murmur of the water soothed and fed her soul. The sun was out today and the warmth felt good on her skin. She sat there, becalmed and still. She reached into her overalls pocket and withdrew a sheet of paper and passed her hand over it, straightening out the crinkles. It had been torn in half at one time and was taped back together. Her fingers traced the lettering. She didn't have to look at it to know what was written there.

Third Grade Mathematics Prize
Awarded to
Amelia Laxault

Her fingers lingered on the gold medallion embossed at the bottom of the document and she smiled. Then, tears fell from her eyes onto the paper and she wiped the paper on her shirt and folded it up again and replaced it in her pocket. For a long time, she sat there and stared at the creek before her, the tears continuing to fall until she was done.

Well Pa, she said, her face lifted to the sky. You were wrong. I found me a man who kisses me when I get hurt.

Finally, she got to her feet. It was time to get home and fix supper.

On the way, she ran through the multiplication tables in her head.

Eight times eight equals…

Acknowledgements

My name is on the cover, but this novel would not have been possible without the help of a lot of other people. Among those I first include Danny Gardner, who said I was the first writer he approached for his new press and signed me before he even signed his own book. In a world with little honor and a trade sometimes rife with egos gone crazy, Danny is that rarity—a true friend and honorable brother.

Also, my agent, Svetlana Pironko, Author's Rights Agency, Dublin/Paris, who is the entire reason this novel was written. She came to me one day, and said one of my short stories, Hard Times, had haunted her ever since she had first read it. She said she thought if I made it the basis of a novel, it had the promise of becoming a story along the lines of a Cormac McCarthy work. I don't know if that happened, but whatever level of excellence it achieved it's because or Svetlana's faith in me.

To my editors, Joe Clifford and Rob Pierce—thank you, guys—you did yeoman work. To Allison Davis who kept all the balls in the air, to Reggie Pulliam, the talented artist who created an amazing cover and Kaye Publicity helping us all, thank you.

CPSIA information can be obtained
at www.ICGtesting.com
Printed in the USA
BVHW041821100121
597497BV00016B/659